Capitalism

Other Books of Related Interest:

At Issue Series

Corporate Corruption

How Can the Poor Be Helped?

Is Socialism Harmful?

Current Controveries Series

Jobs in America

Global Viewpoints Series

Democracy

Issues That Concern You Series

Teens and Employment

Opposing Viewpoints Series

America's Global Influence

Deregulation

Reforming Wall Street

Unemployment

Welfare

GLOBALVIEWPOINTS

Capitalism

Noël Merino, Book Editor

GREENHAVEN PRESS
A part of Gale, Cengage Learning

GALE
CENGAGE Learning

Detroit • New York • San Francisco • New Haven, Conn • Waterville, Maine • London

Elizabeth Des Chenes, *Managing Editor*

© 2012 Greenhaven Press, a part of Gale, Cengage Learning

Gale and Greenhaven Press are registered trademarks used herein under license.

For more information, contact:
Greenhaven Press
27500 Drake Rd.
Farmington Hills, MI 48331-3535
Or you can visit our Internet site at gale.cengage.com

For product information and technology assistance, contact us at

Gale Customer Support, 1-800-877-4253
For permission to use material from this text or product, submit all requests online at
www.cengage.com/permissions

Further permissions questions can be emailed to permissionrequest@cengage.com

Articles in Greenhaven Press anthologies are often edited for length to meet page require-ments. In addition, original titles of these works are changed to clearly present the main thesis and to explicitly indicate the author's opinion. Every effort is made to ensure that Greenhaven Press accurately reflects the original intent of the authors. Every effort has been made to trace the owners of copyrighted material.

Cover image copyright © Paul Brown/Alamy.

LIBRARY OF CONGRESS CATALOGING-IN-PUBLICATION DATA

Capitalism / Noël Merino, book editor.
    p. cm. -- (Global viewpoints)
    Includes bibliographical references and index.
    ISBN 978-0-7377-5646-3 (hbk.) -- ISBN 978-0-7377-5647-0 (pbk.)
  1. Capitalism. I. Merino, Noël.
    HB501.C2422542 2012
    330.12'2--dc23
                                       2011037073

Printed in Mexico
1 2 3 4 5 6 7 16 15 14 13 12

Contents

Chapter 1: Capitalism Around the World

Chapter 2: Capitalism and the Global Financial Crisis

The economic boom and ensuing global financial crisis caused by global capitalism have increased inequalities in developing countries, requiring a new model of capitalism.

Chapter 3: Capitalism and Democracy

Chapter 4: Capitalism and Social Welfare Spending

Instead of calling for a return to the former welfare state, Canadians should be questioning the value of the capitalistic market system that produces large inequalities.

Foreword

Global interdependence has become an undeniable reality. Mass media and technology have increased worldwide access to information and created a society of global citizens. Understanding and navigating this global community is a challenge, requiring a high degree of information literacy and a new level of learning sophistication.

Building on the success of its flagship series, Opposing Viewpoints, Greenhaven Press has created the Global Viewpoints series to examine a broad range of current, often controversial topics of worldwide importance from a variety of international perspectives. Providing students and other readers with the information they need to explore global connections and think critically about worldwide implications, each Global Viewpoints volume offers a panoramic view of a topic of widespread significance.

Drugs, famine, immigration—a broad, international treatment is essential to do justice to social, environmental, health, and political issues such as these. Junior high, high school, and early college students, as well as general readers, can all use Global Viewpoints anthologies to discern the complexities relating to each issue. Readers will be able to examine unique national perspectives while, at the same time, appreciating the interconnectedness that global priorities bring to all nations and cultures.

Material in each volume is selected from a diverse range of sources, including journals, magazines, newspapers, nonfiction books, speeches, government documents, pamphlets, organization newsletters, and position papers. Global Viewpoints is truly global, with material drawn primarily from international sources available in English and secondarily from US sources with extensive international coverage.

Features of each volume in the Global Viewpoints series include:

- An **annotated table of contents** that provides a brief summary of each essay in the volume, including the name of the country or area covered in the essay.

- An **introduction** specific to the volume topic.

- A **world map** to help readers locate the countries or areas covered in the essays.

- For each viewpoint, an **introduction** that contains notes about the author and source of the viewpoint explains why material from the specific country is being presented, summarizes the main points of the viewpoint, and offers three **guided reading questions** to aid in understanding and comprehension.

- **For further discussion** questions that promote critical thinking by asking the reader to compare and contrast aspects of the viewpoints or draw conclusions about perspectives and arguments.

- A worldwide list of **organizations to contact** for readers seeking additional information.

- A **periodical bibliography** for each chapter and a **bibliography of books** on the volume topic to aid in further research.

- A comprehensive **subject index** to offer access to people, places, events, and subjects cited in the text, with the countries covered in the viewpoints highlighted.

Global Viewpoints is designed for a broad spectrum of readers who want to learn more about current events, history, political science, government, international relations, economics, environmental science, world cultures, and sociology— students doing research for class assignments or debates, teachers and faculty seeking to supplement course materials, and others wanting to understand current issues better. By presenting how people in various countries perceive the root causes, current consequences, and proposed solutions to worldwide challenges, Global Viewpoints volumes offer readers opportunities to enhance their global awareness and their knowledge of cultures worldwide.

Introduction

"Despite its severe internal contradictions ... the capitalist system has managed to remain vibrant over the centuries."

—Victor D. Lippit,
Capitalism

Capitalism has recently been under scrutiny due to the global financial crisis that began in the United States in 2007 and quickly spread around the world causing a global recession. Many leaders have criticized American-style capitalism as the ultimate cause of the recession. French president Nicolas Sarkozy told French citizens that the crisis marked the end of laissez-faire capitalism. "A certain idea of globalization is dying with the end of a financial capitalism that had imposed its logic on the whole economy and contributed to perverting it," he is quoted as saying in the *New York Times* in September 2008. Italy's prime minister, Silvio Berlusconi, blamed the financial crisis on a "capitalism of adventurers," according to the *New York Times* on October 12, 2008. Others deny that capitalism caused the crisis. David Boaz, executive vice president of the Cato Institute, said in a January/February 2009 issue of the *Cato Policy Report* that "the crisis can hardly be considered a failure of laissez-faire, deregulation, libertarianism, or capitalism, since it was caused by multiple misguided government interventions into the workings of the financial system. It was and is precisely a failure of interventionism." The debate about whether to embrace a capitalism system and, if so, to what degree is at fever pitch as countries attempt to pull themselves out of the global recession.

Capitalism is an economic system based on private property and free enterprise. This means that nongovernmental private entities own the assets—the land, the resources, the buildings, the technology, and the knowledge—used to create goods and services. Under capitalism, any profits from business go to the private owners of businesses or, in the case of publicly held corporations, their shareholders. Workers, under capitalism, are paid wages for their employment without necessarily having any ownership. There are many competing alternatives to capitalism, the most popular of which are communism and socialism. Capitalism can be starkly contrasted with communism, wherein the means of production and all property are owned in common. Under communism, any wealth created goes back into the common system for the benefit of all. Socialism could be seen as an economic system somewhat in between capitalism and communism. On the one hand, workers may work for a wage and may acquire wealth according to work done, similar to capitalism. On the other hand, the distribution of income is subject to social control by the government. One of socialism's defining features is the role the government plays in controlling the means of production by having a centrally planned economy.

The capitalist mode of production can be traced to England's industrial revolution in the eighteenth century. The big, industrialist countries of the world—the countries of western Europe, Japan, Russia, and the United States—embraced capitalism during the nineteenth century, but during the twentieth century there were several large movements against capitalism, in favor of socialism or communism. The Russian Revolution in 1917 eventually led to the founding of the Union of Soviet Socialist Republics (USSR), which was dominated by the Communist Party until 1990. Similar class struggle revolutions erupted around the globe throughout the early twentieth century, including struggles in Indochina, the Philippines, China, Latin American, and Eastern Europe. By the end of the twentieth century, with the fall of the Soviet Union and other Communist countries, there was a trend toward embracing the market economy to varying degrees.

There are several different forms of capitalism around the world currently. Anglo-American capitalism in the United States, United Kingdom, Canada, Australia, and New Zealand is more individualistic and competitive than European capitalism, for instance. European countries put an emphasis on social decision making and tend to moderate the free market more intensely with a variety of regulations. Japan's version of capitalism has always included strong cooperation between the state and private business toward the goals of prosperity and stability. China has embraced capitalism without abandoning the authoritarianism of its former Communist state. Central and South America moved toward free market economics in the second half of the twentieth century, but privatization of wealth has not resulted in greater economic prosperity for most, causing a backlash toward economic liberalization. Colonial powers in Africa blocked the development of capitalism for indigenous people for quite some time, and in the postcolonial period since the independence struggles in the second half of the twentieth century, instability and corruption have inhibited large-scale economic growth.

Although there is much debate about whether capitalism is a good economic system, even among the proponents of capitalism, a debate rages about the extent to which a capitalist economy should operate within a free market. Capitalist economies throughout the world embrace the free market to varying degrees, and nowhere is there an entirely free market: for instance, there are frequently government regulations on labor, taxes on products and labor, and public ownership of certain services such as utilities. Among critics of capitalism, one can just as easily hear the complaint that any problems in the system are caused by too little government intervention in the market as one can hear the complaint that problems with the system are caused by too much government intervention. This is just one of the ongoing debates about capitalism. By exploring some of these debates—including whether capitalism caused the global financial crisis, the effect of capitalism on democracy, and the degree to which capitalism is compatible with social welfare spending—*Global Viewpoints: Capitalism* helps illuminate some of the most current discussions about capitalism around the world.

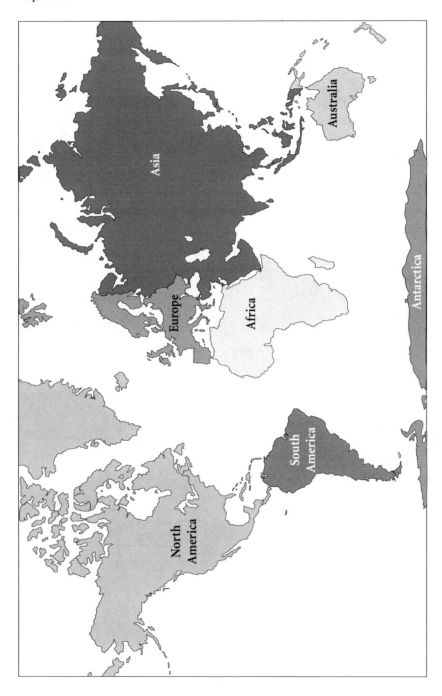

CHAPTER 1

Capitalism Around the World

In France and Germany, Anticapitalist Attitudes Are Widespread

Stefan Theil

*In the following viewpoint, Stefan Theil argues that the perva-
sive anticapitalist sentiment found in France and Germany is
partially attributable to the economics ideology the two countries
teach to schoolchildren. Theil uses examples in support of his
claim that French textbooks emphasize the destruction of capitalism and German textbooks focus on the conflict between employer and employee. He claims that the impact of antimarket
bias in education is a loss of jobs, innovation, and economic success in the two countries. Theil is* Newsweek *magazine's European economics editor.*

As you read, consider the following questions:

1. According to the author, what percent of Germans support socialist ideals?
2. Thiel claims that the one unifying characteristic of German textbooks is the emphasis on what?
3. The author cites a study showing that attitudes explain
   what percent of the variation in start-up and company
   growth rates across nine countries?

Stefan Theil, "Europe's Philosophy of Failure," *Foreign Policy*, no. 164, January/
February 2008, pp. 55–60. Copyright © 2008 by *Foreign Policy*. All rights reserved.
Reproduced by permission.

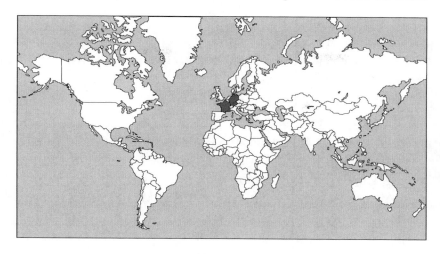

Millions of children are being raised on prejudice and dis-information. Educated in schools that teach a skewed ideology, they are exposed to a dogma that runs counter to core beliefs shared by many other Western countries. They study from textbooks filled with a doctrine of dissent, which they learn to recite as they prepare to attend many of the better universities in the world. Extracting these children from the jaws of bias could mean the difference between world prosperity and menacing global rifts. And doing so will not be easy. But not because these children are found in the *madrasas* [Islamic religious schools] of Pakistan or the state-controlled schools of Saudi Arabia. They are not. Rather, they live in two of the world's great democracies—France and Germany.

The Impact of Economics Lessons

What a country teaches its young people reflects its bedrock national beliefs. Schools hand down a society's historical narrative to the next generation. There has been a great deal of debate over the ways in which this historical ideology is passed on—over Japanese textbooks that downplay the Nanjing Massacre, Palestinian textbooks that feature maps without Israel, and new Russian guidelines that require teachers to portray

Stalinism more favorably. Yet there has been almost no analysis of how countries teach economics, even though the subject is equally crucial in shaping the collective identity that drives foreign and domestic policies.

Just as schools teach a historical narrative, they also pass on "truths" about capitalism, the welfare state, and other economic principles that a society considers self-evident. In both France and Germany, for instance, schools have helped ingrain a serious aversion to capitalism. In one 2005 poll, just 36 percent of French citizens said they supported the free-enterprise system, the only one of 22 countries polled that showed minority support for this cornerstone of global commerce. In Germany, meanwhile, support for socialist ideals is running at all-time highs—47 percent in 2007 versus 36 percent in 1991.

It's tempting to dismiss these attitudes as being little more than punch lines to cocktail party jokes. But their impact is sadly and seriously self-destructive. In Germany, unemployment is finally falling after years at Depression-era levels, thanks in no small part to welfare reforms that in 2005 pressured Germans on the public dole to take up jobs. Yet there is near consensus among Germans that, despite this happy outcome, tinkering with the welfare state went far beyond what is permissible. Chancellor Angela Merkel, once heralded as Germany's own Margaret Thatcher [former British prime minister], has all but abandoned her plans to continue free-market reforms. She has instead imposed a new "rich people tax," has tightened labor-market rules, and has promised renewed efforts to "regulate" globalization. Meanwhile, two in three Germans say they support at least some of the voodoo-economic, roll-back-the-reforms platform of a noisy new antiglobalization political party called Die Linke (The Left), founded by former East German Communists and Western left-wing populists.

Many of these popular attitudes can be traced to state-mandated curricula in schools. It is there that economic lessons are taught that diverge substantially from the market-based principles on which the Western model is based. The phenomenon may hardly be unique to Europe, but in few places is it more obvious than in France and Germany. A biased view of economics feeds into many of the world's most vexing problems, from the growth of populism to the global rise of anti-American, anticapitalist attitudes.

In both France and Germany . . . schools have helped ingrain a serious aversion to capitalism.

French Education on Capitalism

"Economic growth imposes a hectic form of life, producing overwork, stress, nervous depression, cardiovascular disease and, according to some, even the development of cancer," asserts the three-volume *Histoire du XXe siècle*, a set of texts memorized by countless French high school students as they prepare for entrance exams to Sciences Po and other prestigious French universities. The past 20 years have "doubled wealth, doubled unemployment, poverty, and exclusion, whose ill effects constitute the background for a profound social malaise," the text continues. Because the 21st century begins with "an awareness of the limits to growth and the risks posed to humanity [by economic growth]," any future prosperity "depends on the regulation of capitalism on a planetary scale." Capitalism itself is described at various points in the text as "brutal," "savage," "neoliberal," and "American." This agitprop was published in 2005, not in 1972.

When French students are not getting this kind of wildly biased commentary on the destruction wreaked by capitalism, they are learning that economic progress is also the root cause of social ills. For example, a one-year high school course on the inner workings of an economy developed by the French Education Ministry called *Sciences Economiques et Sociales* spends two-thirds of its time discussing the sociopolitical fallout of economic activity. Chapter and section headings include "Social Cleavages and Inequality," "Social Mobilization and Conflict," "Poverty and Exclusion," and "Globalization and Regulation." The ministry mandates that students learn "worldwide regulation as a response" to globalization. Only one-third of the course is about companies and markets, and even those bits include extensive sections on unions, government economic policy, the limits of markets, and the dangers of growth. The overall message is that economic activity has countless undesirable effects from which citizens must be protected.

No wonder, then, that the French default attitude is to be suspicious of market forces and private entrepreneurship, not to mention any policies that would strengthen them. Start-ups, *Histoire du XXe siècle* tells its students, are "audacious enterprises" with "ill-defined prospects." Then it links entrepreneurs with the tech bubble, the Nasdaq crash, and mass layoffs across the economy. (Think "creative destruction" without the "creative.") In one widely used text, a section on technology and innovation does not mention a single entrepreneur or company. Instead, students read a lengthy treatise on whether technological progress destroys jobs. In another textbook, students actually meet a French entrepreneur who invented a new tool to open oysters. But the quirky anecdote is followed by a long-winded debate over the degree to which the modern workplace is organized along the lines imagined by Frederick Taylor, the father of modern scientific management theory. And just in case they missed it in history class, students are reminded that "cultural globalization" leads to violence and armed resistance, ultimately necessitating a new system of global governance.

Economics in US Schools

This is a world apart from what American high school students learn. In the United States, where fewer than half of high school students take an economics course, most classes are based on straightforward, classical economics. In Texas, the state-prescribed curriculum requires that the positive contribution of entrepreneurs to the local economy be taught. The state of New York, meanwhile, has coordinated its curriculum with entrepreneurship-promoting youth groups such as Junior Achievement, as well as with economists at the Federal Reserve. Do American schools encourage students to follow in the footsteps of Bill Gates [the founder of Microsoft] or become ardent fans of globalization? Not really. But they certainly aren't filling students with negative preconceptions and suspicions about businesses and the people who run them. Nor do they obsess about the negative side effects and dangers of economic activity the way French textbooks do.

French students, on the other hand, do not learn economics so much as a very specific, highly biased discourse *about* economics. When they graduate, they may not know much about supply and demand, or about the workings of a corporation. Instead, they will likely know inside-out the evils of "*la McDonaldisation du monde*" and the benefits of a "Tobin tax" [a currency transaction tax] on the movement of global capital. This kind of anticapitalist, antiglobalization discourse isn't just the product of a few aging 1968ers writing for *Le Monde Diplomatique*; it is required learning in today's French schools.

No wonder . . . that the French default attitude is to be suspicious of market forces and private entrepreneurship.

The German Economic Narrative

Germans teach their young people a similar economic narrative, with a slightly different emphasis. The focus is on instilling the corporatist and collectivist traditions of the German system. Although each of Germany's 16 states sets its own education requirements, nearly all teach through the lens of workplace conflict between employer and employee, the cen-

tral battle being over wages and work rules. If there's one unifying characteristic of German textbooks, it's the tremendous
emphasis on group interests, the traditional social-democratic
division of the universe into capital and labor, employer and
employee, boss and worker. Textbooks teach the minutiae of
employer-employee relations, workplace conflict, collective
bargaining, unions, strikes, and worker protection. Even a cur-
sory look at the country's textbooks shows that many are
written from the perspective of a future employee with a
union contract. Bosses and company owners show up in cari-
catures and illustrations as idle, cigar-smoking plutocrats;
sometimes linked to child labor, Internet fraud, cell-phone addiction, alcoholism, and, of course, undeserved layoffs. The
successful, modern entrepreneur is virtually nowhere to be
found.

German students will be well versed in many subjects
upon graduation; one topic they will know particularly well is
their rights as welfare recipients. One 10th-grade social studies
text titled FAKT has a chapter on "What to do against unemployment." Instead of describing how companies might create
jobs, the section explains how those without jobs can organize
into self-help groups and join weekly antireform protests "in
the tradition of the East German Monday demonstrations"
(which in 1989 helped topple the Communist dictatorship).
The not-so-subtle subtext? Jobs are a right to be demanded
from the government. The same chapter also details various
welfare programs, explains how employers use the threat of
layoffs as a tactic to cut pay, and concludes with a long ex-
cerpt from the platform of the German [Trade] Union Fed-
eration, including the 30-hour work week, retirement at age
60, and redistribution of the work pie by splitting full-time
into part-time jobs. No market alternative is taught. When
FAKT presents the reasons for unemployment, it blames com-
puters and robots. In fact, this is a recurring theme in Ger-

man textbooks—the Internet will turn workers into "anonymous code" and kill off interpersonal communication.

Equally popular in Germany today are student workbooks on globalization. One such workbook includes sections headed "The Revival of Manchester Capitalism," "The Brazilianization of Europe," and "The Return of the Dark Ages." India and China are successful, the book explains, because they have large, state-owned sectors and practice protectionism, while the societies with the freest markets lie in impoverished sub-Saharan Africa. Like many French and German books, this text suggests students learn more by contacting the antiglobalization group Attac, best known for organizing messy protests at the annual G8 [a forum for eight major world economies] summits.

If there's one unifying characteristic of German textbooks, it's the tremendous emphasis on group interests.

The Impact of the Antimarket Bias

One might expect Europeans to view the world through a slightly left-of-center, social-democratic lens. The surprise is the intensity and depth of the antimarket bias being taught in Europe's schools. Students learn that private companies destroy jobs while government policy creates them. Employers exploit while the state protects. Free markets offer chaos while government regulation brings order. Globalization is destructive, if not catastrophic. Business is a zero-sum game, the source of a litany of modern social problems. Some enterprising teachers and parents may try to teach an alternative view, and some books are less ideological than others. But given the biases inherent in the curricula, this background is unavoidable. It is the context within which most students develop intellectually. And it's a belief system that must eventually appear to be the truth.

This bias has tremendous implications that reach far beyond the domestic political debate in these two countries. These beliefs inform students' choices in life. Taught that the free market is a dangerous wilderness, twice as many Germans as Americans tell pollsters that you should not start a business if you think it might fail. According to the European Union's internal polling, just two in five Germans and French would like to be their own boss, compared to three in five Americans. Whereas 8 percent of Americans say they are currently involved in starting a business, that's true of only 2 percent of Germans and 1 percent of the French. Another 28 percent of Americans are considering starting a business, compared to just 11 percent of the French and 18 percent of Germans. The loss to Europe's two largest economies in terms of jobs, innovation, and economic dynamism is severe.

Attitudes and mind-sets, it is increasingly being shown, are closely related to a country's economic performance. Edmund Phelps, a Columbia University economist and Nobel laureate, contends that attitudes toward markets, work, and risk-taking are significantly more powerful in explaining the variation in countries' actual economic performance than the traditional factors upon which economists focus, including social spending, tax rates, and labor-market regulation. The connection between capitalism and culture, once famously described by Max Weber, also helps explain continental Europe's poor record in entrepreneurship and innovation. A study by the Massachusetts-based Monitor Group, the entrepreneurship benchmarking index, looks at nine countries and finds a powerful correlation between attitudes about economics and actual corporate performance. The researchers find that attitudes explain 40 percent of the variation in start-up and company growth rates—by far the strongest correlation of any of the 31 indicators they tested. If countries such as France and Germany hope to boost entrepreneurship, innovation, and economic dynamism—as their leaders claim they do—the

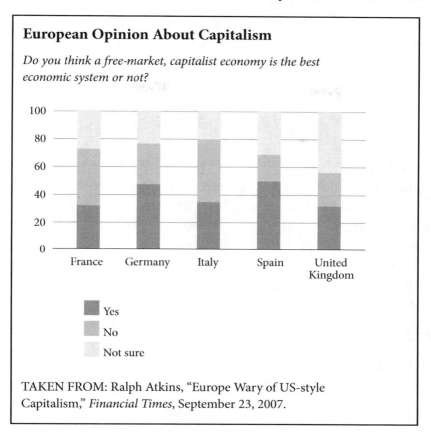

European Opinion About Capitalism

Do you think a free-market, capitalist economy is the best economic system or not?

Legend:
- Yes
- No
- Not sure

TAKEN FROM: Ralph Atkins, "Europe Wary of US-style Capitalism," *Financial Times*, September 23, 2007.

most effective way to make that happen may be to use education to boost the cultural legitimacy of going into business.

A Deeply Held Economic Ideology

The deep antimarket bias that French and Germans continue to teach challenges the conventional wisdom that it's just a matter of time, thanks to the pressures of globalization, before much of the world agrees upon a supposedly "Western" model of free-market capitalism. Politicians in democracies cannot long fight the preferences of the majority of their constituents. So this bias will likely continue to circumscribe both European elections and policy outcomes. A likely alternative scenario may be that the changes wrought by globalization will awaken deeply held resentment against capitalism and, in many countries from Europe to Latin America, provide a fertile ground for populists and demagogues, a trend that is already manifesting itself in the sudden rise of many leftist movements today.

Minimal reforms to the welfare state cost former German chancellor Gerhard Schröder his job in 2005. They have also paralyzed modern German politics. Former Communists and disaffected Social Democrats, together with left-wing Greens, have flocked to Germany's new leftist party, whose politics is a distasteful mix of anticapitalist demagoguery and right-wing xenophobia. Its platform, polls show, is finding support even among mainstream Germans. A left-leaning majority, within both the parliament and the public at large, makes the world's third-largest economy vulnerable to destructive policies driven by anticapitalist resentment and fear of globalization. Similar situations are easily conceivable elsewhere and have already helped bring populists to power in Latin America. Then there is France, where President Nicolas Sarkozy promised to "rupture" with the failed economic policies of the past. He has taken on the country's public servants and their famously lavish benefits, but many of his policies appear to be driven by what he calls "economic patriotism," which smacks of old-fashioned industrial protectionism. That's exactly what French schoolchildren have long learned is the way the world should work.

Both the French and German cases show the limits of trying to run against the grain of deeply held economic ideology. Yet, training the next generation of citizens to be prejudiced against being enterprising and productive is equally foolhardy. Fortunately, such widespread attitudes and the political outcomes they foster aren't only determined by tradition and history. They are, to a great extent, the product of education. If countries like France and Germany hope to get their nations on a new economic track, they might start paying more attention to what their kids are learning in the classroom.

Scandinavian Countries Practice a Superior Form of Capitalism

Dominique Moisi

In the following viewpoint, Dominique Moisi argues that Scandinavia offers a political, economic, social, and ethical model that should be emulated by the rest of Europe. Moisi claims that the positive results of Scandinavian capitalism are evident in economic performance, social climate, and the political culture of the region. Moisi contends that for Europe's model of capitalism to be a model for China and elsewhere, it needs to reflect the values of Scandinavian capitalism. Moisi is founder and senior advisor at the French Institute of International Relations and a professor at the College of Europe in Natolin, Poland.

As you read, consider the following questions:

1. What two virtues does the author use to describe political power in Scandinavia?
2. Moisi claims that the weak countries in Europe in terms of economic performance, social climate, and political culture are in what region?
3. According to Moisi, China is increasingly becoming what for Europe?

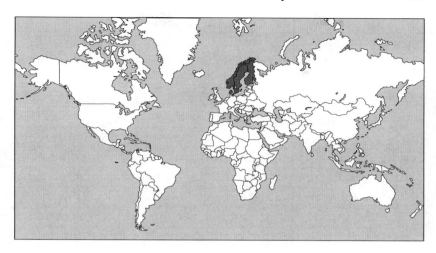

The Northern Lights was the title of a major painting exhibition in Paris . . . dedicated to Scandinavian masterpieces. But "northern lights" may also correspond to what Europe, if not the entire West, needs nowadays: a political, economic, social, and ethical model. Indeed, in becoming the first centre-right leader in Sweden to win re-election in modern times, Prime Minister Fredrik Reinfeldt not only ended the centre-left's electoral hegemony in his country, but revealed that the modern Scandinavian model of governance is relevant across Europe.

The Scandinavian Virtues

At a time when budget cuts are the order of the day, political power in Scandinavia is modest and generally honest. Women play a major role in society and politics, and have for a long time. Scandinavian capitalism has been traditionally more humane, and social injustice, though it exists, is much less destructive than in southern Europe, for example. Moreover, immigrants are generally treated with a greater sense of respect for their dignity.

To be sure, many other Europeans recognize these "virtues." But their natural reaction is to say, "It's not for us." In order to practice Scandinavian virtues, many believe, you must come from a cold-weather country with a small, homogeneous population that accepts high taxes without grumbling.

One can behave in such a manner, many Europeans outside of Scandinavia say, only if one has been raised according to the Protestant ethic. For Greeks, Italians, and many French, evading taxes is a kind of national pastime, which some even perceive as a moral duty. Politics is a game, and power a drug that allows you to rise above ordinary citizens. And the temptation to consider oneself the incarnation of the state, rather than its servant, is often irresistible among southern European politicians.

Scandinavian capitalism has been traditionally more humane.

Of course, it is dangerous to idealize the Scandinavian model. Scandinavian countries have their share of problems, such as Denmark's significant xenophobic extreme right and Norway's occasional bouts of provincial puritanism.

But the difference between these countries and their southern counterparts in terms of economic performance, social climate, and political culture are plainly visible. The weak and sick men of Europe—from Greece to Spain—are to be found in the south, not the north.

The Asian Challenge

The Asian challenge, particularly from China, should encourage us to reconsider the validity of the "Scandinavian model." For the Chinese example represents for Europeans a dual opportunity to moralize our capitalism and reinvent our democratic practices. We cannot continue to preach to others values that we no longer practice with rigor. To play the moral high ground, we must deserve it.

The Nordic Model of Capitalism

The model of capitalism practised in Sweden, Norway, Denmark and Finland is seen by some as one of the few winners of the current economic and financial crisis. From its response to a previous banking crisis to its promotion of women in the boardroom, the Nordic model is piquing interest around the world in the same way as the Japanese style of capitalism did in the 1980s or the Germans' in the 1960s.

Richard Milne and Andrew Ward, "Illuminating Outline,"
Financial Times, *July 29, 2009.*

Moreover, we cannot simply wait for the Chinese "other" to collapse under the weight of its own contradictions. Of course, these contradictions are real, but our main source of strength cannot be their weakness. The Chinese model—inspired nowadays not by [Russian revolutionary Vladimir] Lenin but by Singapore's decades of disciplined economic success—has called into question the traditional linkage (made since [18th-century Scottish social philosopher] Adam Smith) between capitalism and democracy.

In China, capitalism prospers without democracy. In fact, a contemporary Chinese joke is very indicative of how the country perceives its role in today's world. "In 1949, communism saved China; in 1979 capitalism saved China; and in 2009, China saved capitalism."

Regaining Universal Attractiveness

In the aftermath of a major financial and economic crisis—which may yet be far from over—Chinese and Asians in general ask Europeans rather bluntly how we dare try to teach them lessons in financial capitalism. After all, during the Asian financial crisis in 1998, "we" did not come to their aid; ten years later, "they" saved us.

China today is increasingly becoming for Europe what the United States was yesterday—a mirror reflecting our weaknesses and our strengths. We are too few to become anything other than a "niche of excellence" in the character of our capitalism and our democratic practices, both of which are endangered above all by ourselves.

Looking north is essential if we want to regain our universal attractiveness and defend our "democratic" comparative advantages.

Nothing incites failure more than success. Since the end of the Cold War, we Europeans have lost the incentive to demonstrate the superiority of our systems. We have become complacent and lazy.

In this context, looking north is essential if we want to regain our universal attractiveness and defend our "democratic" comparative advantages. There is more rigor and openness under the Northern Lights, and this is precisely the combination we need, with its mixture of modesty towards others and ambition towards ourselves.

Popular Opinion in China Favors Capitalism

James A. Dorn

In the following viewpoint, James A. Dorn argues that recent surveys show that the vast majority of Chinese favor capitalism, with the components of a free market economy, as well as increased globalization and international trade. Dorn claims that China's move toward capitalism has increased wealth in China and around the world. Nonetheless, Dorn contends that China needs to take further steps to increase the free market by embracing the will of the people and minimizing the interference by the state. Dorn is a China specialist at the Cato Institute and professor of economics at Towson University in Maryland.

As you read, consider the following questions:

1. According to Dorn, a recent poll found that what percent of people in China agreed that the free market economy is the best system?

2. The author claims that what percent of Chinese believe that international trade is good for the job security of workers?

3. Dorn concludes that in order for the free market to work in China, economic freedom must be coupled with what other kind of freedom?

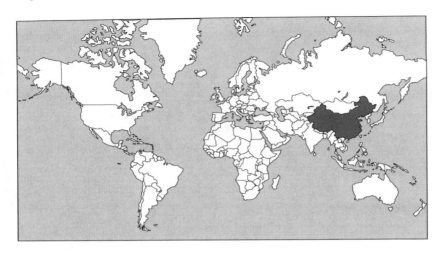

In a 2005 poll covering 20 countries, GlobeScan found that China had the highest proportion of respondents (74%) agree that the "free market economy is the best system on which to base the future of the world." That outcome is remarkable given that only a short time ago (prior to 1979) Beijing embraced a state-led development model.

The same poll found that US citizens have strong support for the free market (71%) while Russia, which has a long anti-capitalist history, still has rather weak support (43% favoured the market), and France, with its long attachment to socialism, has even less support with only 36% saying they favour a free market.

The significant change in attitude toward capitalism in China is further illustrated by the Chicago Council on Global Affairs' 2006 multination survey of public opinion. Eighty-seven percent of those surveyed in China thought that "globalisation, especially the increasing connections of their country's economy with others around the world, is mostly good for their country." That result compares with 60% in the United States and 54% in India.

It is not surprising that the Chinese people would embrace globalisation as it has opened China to the outside world, brought about rapid economic and social change, and helped lift millions out of absolute poverty. In widening the range of opportunities open to people, globalisation has put pressure on the Chinese Communist Party (CCP) to allow privatisation and marketisation—with a positive impact on civil society. People are able to own their own homes, operate their own businesses, and seek work in the private sector.

Trade liberalisation has been good for China and good for the global economy. Even though millions of Chinese workers have been dislocated, the Chicago Council survey found that 65% of those polled in China believe that "international trade is good for the job security of workers." In contrast, only 30% of Americans surveyed thought free international trade benefited workers.

Of course, the goal of trade is not to protect jobs but to create wealth—and global wealth is much greater today than it was two or three decades ago. Trade liberalisation, the information revolution, and financial integration have combined with pro-market institutional change to make China's—and the global economy's—future bright.

Trade liberalisation has been good for China and good for the global economy.

One lesson from China's transition from central planning to a market-oriented system is that poverty is best addressed by institutional change rather than foreign aid and government intervention. Several decades ago most of the world's poor were concentrated in Asia, not Africa. The reverse is true today. Foreign aid has not improved the plight of the poor.

Likewise, increasing the minimum wage is not a panacea. Politicians promise a higher wage but do nothing to address the underlying causes of poverty. Rather, if the legal minimum wage is above the prevailing market wage for unskilled work-

---

Entrepreneurship in China

The spirit of entrepreneurship is evident everywhere in China. One of the most popular TV game shows is *Win in China*, a contest in which the person with the best business plan is awarded venture capital financing of $1.2 million and gets to retain 20 percent of the equity. The first show in 2006 attracted 120,000 entrants. The host of the show, Anna Wang Lifen, launched the program because she sees entrepreneurs as "the heroes of our peaceful times."

James A. Dorn, "Adam Smith in China:
The Momentum for Market Liberalization in China Is Strong,"
Freeman, vol. 57, no. 4, May 2007.

---

ers, employers will cut back on hours, reduce benefits, and switch to labour-saving methods of production.

Hong Kong has no minimum wage, yet is prosperous. China has no national minimum wage and lets the market guide local minimum wages so that they do not interfere with job growth. In Shenzhen, the minimum wage was increased last year [2006] to 810 yuan per month, but the local labour official Wu Liyong, said, "We are adapting to the market through the pay raise, rather than interfering with the market." Many companies already pay more than the minimum, and there is a labour shortage so that market wages will be forced up by competition.

Although China has made substantial progress on its march toward the market, much remains to be done. Free markets require widespread private property rights, a transparent and just legal system, and the free flow of information. Moreover, if China is to develop world-class capital markets, Beijing must make the yuan fully convertible and allow capital freedom. Opening the CCP [Chinese Communist Party] to capitalists is not sufficient. The Party's monopoly on power has to be contested at some point. Nor is it sufficient to amend the PRC [People's Republic of China] Constitution to better protect private property when there is no independent judiciary to enforce contracts.

If China's future is to rest with the free market, there must be political as well as economic liberalisation.

The National People's Congress is expected to pass a new law in March [2007] to further strengthen private property rights. But the law will have no teeth unless there is also meaningful judicial reform, which appears unlikely in a one-party state.

If China's future is to rest with the free market, there must be political as well as economic liberalisation. Ultimately, a free market cannot exist without a free people. The real challenge for Beijing will be to institute a rule of law that protects persons and property against the state. The people's preferences will then rule rather than the Party's.

In Russia, So-Called Kremlin Capitalism Is Fascism, Not Capitalism

Peter Foster

In the following viewpoint, Peter Foster argues that it is a mistake to claim that Russia practices any kind of capitalism. Recounting the imprisonment of a Russian oil oligarch, Foster claims that the interference by the government in business makes capitalism impossible. He contends that just because private business exists, there is no adherence to the ideal of capitalism if private businesses must make deals with an authoritarian government in order to operate. Foster is a columnist for the Financial Post, *the business section of the* National Post, *a Canadian newspaper.*

As you read, consider the following questions:

1. What three kinds of so-called capitalism does Foster claim are in fact negations of capitalism?

2. What reason does the author give for claiming that Mikhail Khodorkovsky should not be compared with Cornelius Vanderbilt, Andrew Carnegie, and John D. Rockefeller?

3. Foster claims that a system in which private business must cooperate with authoritarian government is called what?

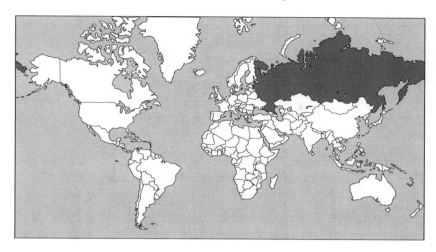

Mikhail Khodorkovsky's additional six years in the Siberian slammer confirms—if any further confirmation is needed—that the rule of law means nothing in [Prime Minister] Vladimir Putin's Russia. It is galling, however, that Mr. Putin's thuggish regime is constantly referred to as "Kremlin capitalism," "state capitalism," or "crony capitalism."

Kremlinism, statism, and cronyism are all in fact negations of capitalism, which is a system based on private property and the rule of law. Government is needed to protect the system, but that does not mean that it is compatible with anything that government chooses to do.

Unless people understand what rightly defined capitalism is—as opposed to the demonic parody of greed and exploitation crafted by [German political philosopher Karl] Marx and more recently gussied up with accusations of environmental fecklessness—it becomes impossible to defend or promote.

Business and Politics in Russia

It has, for example, been suggested that Mr. Khodorkovsky and his fellow oligarchs were analogous to those great capitalists who were dubbed "robber barons"—men such as Cornelius Vanderbilt, Andrew Carnegie and John D. Rockefeller—

but the comparison is utterly invalid. Messrs. Vanderbilt, Carnegie and Rockefeller built great commercial enterprises from scratch and brought enormous benefits by slashing the costs, respectively, of travel, steel and lighting. They didn't seize great slabs of assets from a collapsed Communist state at knock-down prices, even if, as in the case of Mr. Khodorkovsky, he then proceeded enormously to enhance the value of those assets.

Mr. Khodorkovsky first attracted Mr. Putin's ire in 2003, when he made the mistake of challenging the then Russian president. Mr. Putin—a former secret police chief who had taken over as president from the pickled Boris Yeltsin in 2000—was affronted because Mr. Khodorkovsky's challenge reputedly breached an "agreement" with the oligarchs that Mr. Putin would stay out of business if they would stay out of politics. But Mr. Putin was never going to stay out of business.

There were aspects of Mr. Khodorkovsky's corporate strategy that were profoundly unappealing to Russian nationalists. He was planning to sell a major stake in Yukos to ExxonMobil (the main inheritor of Mr. Rockefeller's Standard Oil). Mr. Putin clearly regarded Yukos as "strategic": that is, if it wasn't owned locally, it couldn't be so easily controlled. But Mr. Putin had something a little more muscular in mind than Saskatchewan Premier Brad Wall had for PotashCorp. He wanted to control the Russian oil industry as a generator of revenue to make Russia, "great" again. That is, feared.

The Continued Political Thuggery

In the wake of the Yukos seizure and Mr. Khodorkovsky's alleged crime and very real punishment, Mr. Putin proceeded to flex his political muscle by shaking down the major foreign oil companies who had looked to Russia to boost supplies. He was all the more successful because the price of oil surged in the four years after his assault on Yukos, peaking in 2008, the year Mr. Putin was forced to cede the presidency. Although

"Putin Kind of Capitalism," cartoon by Mike Lane and www.CagleCartoons.com, September 26, 2008. Copyright © 2008 by Mike Lane and www.CagleCartoons.com. All rights reserved. Reproduced by permission.

Mr. Putin became prime minister, there were hopes that the new president, Dmitry Medvedev, might be something more than a puppet. He isn't.

When Mr. Putin first took down Mr. Khodorkovsky in 2003, the Russian stock market fell 10%. It was hoped that the possible investment consequences of political thuggery might restrain him. However, the rising price of oil, the amorality of Western investors, and the "courting" of Mr. Putin by European politicians who wanted him to ratify the Kyoto accord [referring to the Kyoto Protocol, an agreement between nations dealing with global warming], not to mention U.S. President Barack Obama's more recent eagerness to shake hands with devils, has left him virtually free rein.

Last summer [2010], the powers of the secret police were expanded, and in October Mr. Putin gave police permission to "crack heads with batons" if people protested "illegally." It is a tribute to the bravery of many Russians that they continue to do so—with Mr. Khodorkovsky as their inspiration and focus—despite the threatened violence.

Fascism, Not Capitalism

Russia produces 10 million barrels a day, more than any other country. This "oil curse" has meant that Mr. Putin's petro-tyranny has become a place where crusaders are frequently bumped off. This may fit Hollywood's image of capitalism, but not the reality, which, to reiterate, is about security of property, the rule of law, and voluntary relationships. Just because there is "private" business in Russia, and individual capitalists are allowed to operate there, that certainly doesn't make it capitalism.

> *Just because there is "private" business in Russia, and individual capitalists are allowed to operate there, that certainly doesn't make it capitalism.*

In the wake of the first Yukos trial, some businessmen suggested—in their ignorance, and to their shame—that Russia might benefit from a little "benevolent dictatorship." Bankers and consultants lined up to lend legitimacy to the "transfer" of Yukos to state hands. Big oil companies—who have spent their existence dealing with unsavoury regimes—looked at Russia in terms of risk analysis rather than morality, preferring to demonstrate their ethical sensitivity in solar panel research.

Many people understandably fail to grasp that capitalism is not necessarily what is either practised or preached by capitalists. Capitalism is an ideal, but unlike the socialism of state control it is an attainable, and moral, one. A system in which private business must co-operate with authoritarian government is called fascism. Historically, fascism and communism were both rooted in hatred of capitalism. "Kremlin capitalism" is an Orwellian contradiction [destructive to the welfare of a free society, according to author George Orwell].

Africa Is Undergoing a Capitalist Revolution That Must Continue

Ethan B. Kapstein

In the following viewpoint, Ethan B. Kapstein argues that Africa has been undergoing a capitalist revolution that has led to economic growth and political progress. Kapstein claims that urbanization, increased communication, and openness have forced African countries to become more globally competitive and democratized. Kapstein contends that because foreign investment and foreign trade have driven Africa's capitalist revolution, it would be a mistake for Europe and North America to engage in protectionist policies that could halt the beneficial revolution. Kapstein is a professor of economics and political science at INSEAD, an international graduate business school, and author of Sharing the Wealth: Workers and the World Economy.

As you read, consider the following questions:

1. Kapstein claims that international trade accounts for what percent of Africa's gross domestic product (GDP)?

2. According to the author, what percent of Africans now live in cities?

3. What percent of cases of democratization in Africa have failed between 1960 and 2004, according to Kapstein?

Ethan B. Kapstein, "Africa's Capitalist Revolution: Preserving Growth in a Time of Crisis," *Foreign Affairs*, vol. 88, no. 4, July/August 2009, pp. 119–128. Copyright © 2009 by *Foreign Affairs*. All rights reserved. Reproduced by permission.

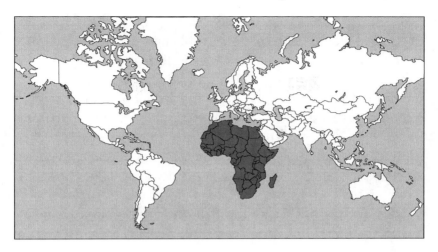

In one of the great ironies of history, Africa may well emerge from the current global recession as the only region in the world that remains committed to global capitalism. While the tired industrialized nations of the West are nationalizing their banks and engaging in various forms of protectionism, Africa remains open for business—promoting trade, foreign direct investment, and domestic entrepreneurship. Analysts in the industrialized countries are concerned that foreign aid flows to Africa might drop because of the recession, but Africans themselves are much more worried about rising barriers to their exports and diminishing private investment from abroad, which could impede the continuation of the impressive economic progress the continent has made over the past decade.

Economic Growth in Africa

It is still a well-kept secret that the African continent has been in the midst of a profound economic transformation. Since 2004, economic growth has boomed at an average level of 6 percent annually, on par with Latin America. This rate will undoubtedly decline as a result of the global financial crisis, but the International Monetary Fund still projects growth of around 1.5 percent for this year [2009] and 4 percent for 2010 throughout Africa—a relatively healthy figure by today's depressing standards. International trade now accounts for nearly 60 percent of Africa's GDP [gross domestic product] (far above the level for Latin America), and foreign direct investment in Africa has more than doubled since 1998, to over $15 billion per year. Overall, private-sector investment constitutes more than 20 percent of GDP. Furthermore, since 1990, the number of countries with stock markets in sub-Saharan Africa has tripled and the capitalization of those exchanges has risen from virtually nothing to $245 billion (that is, outside of South Africa, which has long had an active stock exchange). These "frontier" markets have, until recently, given investors huge returns compared to those found in other emerging economies.

But these positive trends may not last. Bad governments in Africa—often tribal in their orientation, with Kenya being a notable example—have long rewarded insiders and engaged in widespread corruption and often even the outright theft of national resources. In such regimes, military officials and dictators have generally monopolized economic activity, providing few, if any, incentives for legitimate entrepreneurs to do business. It comes as no surprise that under these circumstances Africa suffered from low growth rates and high levels of poverty.

Political Changes in Africa

Far-reaching political changes since 1990, however, have played a crucial role in Africa's capitalist revolution. With the tragic exception of Zimbabwe, one finds widespread progress alongside the economic transformation. In January 2009, Ghana held a crucial presidential election that led to its second peaceful transfer of power in a decade, an event that was widely celebrated across the continent. Even where democracy remains fragile, as in Kenya, leaders understand that the old patrimonial ways of doing business are becoming increasingly costly to maintain. Anticorruption commissions of varying degrees of effectiveness are springing up in a growing number of countries, with Cameroon being one example. Citizens are also demanding more competent leaders who are capable of governing modern societies integrated into a global economy. For example, after being democratically elected in 2006, the president of Benin, Thomas Yayi Boni, emphasized that his cabinet would consist of "technocrats," recruited from universities and development banks. And in Liberia, a former World Bank official, Ellen Johnson Sirleaf, became president in 2006.

But given the continent's many chronic problems, these changes are not necessarily durable, and they could easily be reversed by the current crisis and rising protectionism in the West. If Africa does not do more to encourage entrepreneurship, and if the current great recession leads to a significant reduction in foreign capital flows and higher trade barriers in the United States and western Europe, then the region's nascent capitalist revolution could meet an untimely demise.

Africa's Capitalist Revolution

During the 1990s, just as Africa was laying the groundwork for its current growth spurt, many Western experts and policy makers were busy writing off the continent's future. But the generalized failure to predict Africa's capitalist revolution should come as no surprise. The end of the Cold War [a period of tension between the United States and the Soviet Union in the second half of the twentieth century] meant that Africa was no longer a focal point for the U.S.-Soviet struggle, and the continent lost the strategic significance it had once enjoyed. Oil prices were low, and the region's economies seemed hopeless. They were commodity—and aid—dependent at a time when the revenue streams from each of these sources were falling, and they were mired in billions of dollars of debt to Western governments and banks. To the extent that anyone cared about Africa, it was the foreign aid community.

Donors and humanitarian organizations—driven in part by a desire to ensure continued flows of foreign aid—painted a relentlessly bleak picture of a region beset by hunger, disease, violent civil conflict, huge debt burdens, and corrupt and dysfunctional governments.

Yet behind this facade, Africa's economic potential was stirring. At home, Africa was urbanizing and democratizing, and internationally, the continent was opening up to global trade, forcing its economies to become more competitive. Together, these changes provided the background conditions for the region's capitalist revolution.

The Importance of Urbanization

Urbanization is one trend that development economists seem to ignore when making their forecasts. That is striking, because more than 30 percent of all Africans now live in cities—up from 15 percent in 1965—a number that should rise to over 50 percent of the population in the next 20 or 30 years (a percentage comparable to that in Asia, a region that most people think of as exceptionally urbanized). The shift from rural to urban life is crucial for galvanizing economic development because cities bring people with goods and ideas together with those who have capital. This interaction is the foundation of a market economy. But the pathway to the market requires an additional step beyond mere networking. Trading also requires something that is incredibly risky: engaging in exchanges with people who are not family members or personal friends. In markets, people agree to trade with those they do not know, and that requires a major act of faith.

In Africa, one great virtue of urbanization is that it has forced members of different tribes to interact on a regular basis in ways that remain unusual in more rural settings. These continuous interactions, whether in small shops, on buses, in dwellings, or in the workplace, are absolutely crucial to the development of market economies and democratic institutions, because they help break down patrimonial exchange relationships, in which local chiefs basically run a command economy. As economies become more complex due to urbanization, new skills, such as finance, become valuable; possession of these skills becomes more important than ethnicity when it comes to survival.

The shift from rural to urban life is crucial for galvanizing economic development.

These urban areas are also great centers of economic activity, and their citizens naturally seek to stay informed about what is going on around them. Cell phones and the Internet have made the outside world increasingly accessible to Africans, with far-reaching consequences for economic and political life. Since 2000, growth in cell-phone usage has been greater in Africa than in any other region of the world: It has increased tenfold, to about 80 million subscribers. Internet growth has been even more impressive: The number of people with Internet access has quadrupled since 2000. Still, only a small fraction of the African population today has access to cell phones or the Internet. But this "digital divide" is closing fast, and the economic effects in terms of greater opportunity are already being felt by every would-be or already established entrepreneur. The World Bank has shown, for example, how cell phones have helped farmers gain quicker access to market prices, enabling them to sell their crops for a greater profit.

Openness and Democratization

Enhanced communication between Africa and the world at large has had implications for governments as well. For much of the postcolonial era, dictatorial African governments implemented extremely severe protectionist trade and investment policies, a practice that was aided and abetted by protectionism in the industrialized world. The African business class was deprived of cutting-edge technology at home and denied access to foreign capital and markets overseas. As a result, the continent was shaken by numerous economic crises during the 1980s. In recent years, however, Africa has been able to reap many of globalization's commercial benefits without paying all the financial costs, because its banking sector has been relatively sheltered from international financial markets. Of course, as the continent becomes more enmeshed in the world economy, it will be less able to isolate itself from future financial shocks.

Throughout the 1990s, as Africa urbanized and adopted modern communications technology, the costs associated with those old policies became increasingly apparent. African entrepreneurs—and there were a few scattered about—came to understand that they simply could not build businesses in the small and primitive markets in their own countries; as [18th-century Scottish social philosopher] Adam Smith taught, sustained growth requires the expansion of the market. During the 1990s, "openness" became a watchword for this small entrepreneurial class: It meant the liberalization and privatization of domestic activities once firmly controlled by governments, along with globalization of the marketplace.

Openness also meant political change, however; in particular, it forced governments to take a fresh look at democratization. Very few people today would opt to live in Zimbabwe over Ghana. Indeed, most Africans who still live in authoritarian countries probably hope for a democratic future, even if its realization may be decades away. Because African societies are generally divided along tribal lines and the dominant tribe tends to monopolize resource wealth, pluralism in African politics—along with a system of effective checks and balances—is essential to sustained growth. In contrast to the countries of East Asia, which have done reasonably well under authoritarian regimes, Africa has generally done poorly, and its unelected rulers now have little credibility left with the majority of the people of their countries. This is because Africa's autocrats are for the most part tribal leaders concerned only with bettering the lives of their kin. The recent election in Ghana, marking one of the very few times in African history in which a peaceful transition of power has taken place, may someday be regarded as the decisive turning point when democracy finally took unshakable root in that country. To be sure, Africa has seen many false dawns when it comes to political reform, but the pressures—both domestic and international—in support of greater democracy are rising. Domestically, political parties are growing stronger, and internationally, numerous foreign aid programs have included funds for democracy building. Additional sources of change from outside the continent have come as a result of greater openness to the world economy. Therefore, Africans are looking at the Western world's response to the financial crisis with a high degree of anxiety. . . .

Africa's Dependence on Foreign Capital and Trade

The future of Africa's development hinges on whether the continent will be able to complete its capitalist revolution or the tidal wave of problems created by the global economic crisis will drown the hopes of the region's entrepreneurs. A recent study by the Center for Global Development found that Africa's private sector was all too often impeded by poor infrastructure, small markets, and weak governance. The study also found that ethnic fragmentation remains a divisive factor in economic and political life throughout Africa. However, as mentioned above, Africa is experiencing a major trend toward urbanization, which could help overcome this impediment to growth. But until its ethnic divisions are surmounted, Africa is unlikely to see the rise in productivity that is the *sine qua non* [essential element] of income growth.

Despite some recent success stories, democracy also continues to struggle on the African continent. Young democracies in Africa have had a higher failure rate than those in any other developing region, with nearly 30 percent of all cases of democratization between 1960 and 2004 ending in collapse. On a more hopeful note, however, Africa's successful democracies have become increasingly stable, thanks in part to the foreign aid that has been targeted at strengthening nascent democratic institutions. This aid has built up the capacity of judiciaries and parliaments and bolstered political parties, universities, and a free press.

The future of Africa's development hinges on whether the continent will be able to complete its capitalist revolution.

Even with strengthened democratic institutions, African countries may not be able to withstand the economic pressure from abroad given Africa's growing dependence on foreign capital and trade. Everywhere, countries are beginning to batten down the economic hatches, closing off their economies to foreign trade through a variety of insidious policy measures. Protectionist policies that currently prevent African farmers from exporting genetically modified crops to the European Union [EU] are likely to harden in the months ahead as EU leaders attempt to appease their domestic agricultural sector.

The Need to Avoid Protectionism

Trade is critical to Africa's economic growth, because Africans' incomes cannot rise if their countries are unable to export goods and services to richer regions. To be sure, African countries themselves must do more to create free-trade zones and promote commerce with other developing nations. But in the end, it is the wealthy consumers of Europe and North America whose buying power will lift Africans out of poverty. For Europe and the United States, protectionism and reduced trade are merely costly, at least for now; but for Africa, with its small domestic markets, they are potentially deadly.

It is hard to imagine Barack Obama—a U.S. president of Kenyan descent—leveling such a cruel blow against his ancestral homeland. Yet although the Obama administration was tireless in warning of a domestic catastrophe if Congress did not pass an economic stimulus package and a bailout for U.S. banks, it has been relatively silent when it comes to warning of the international catastrophe that would accompany a renewed round of protectionist policies. The "Buy American" provision of the stimulus package that President Obama signed into law—which he has defended as being consistent with the rules of the World Trade Organization—exposes the absurdity of developed-world governments that give with one hand by promoting economic development and take with the other by practicing protectionism. Africans have already taken up the shovel to dig themselves out of a half-century-old hole of poor economic management and bad governance. It is now up to the United States and its European allies to help them complete the job.

Periodical and Internet Sources Bibliography

The following articles have been selected to supplement the diverse views presented in this chapter.

Anders Aslund	"The Death of Putin's Crony Capitalism," *Jakarta Globe*, February 28, 2010.
Ralph Atkins	"Europe Wary of US-Style Capitalism," *Financial Times*, September 23, 2007.
Zaher Bitar	"Capitalism Still the System of Choice," *Gulf News* (Dubai, United Arab Emirates), January 14, 2011.
Ian Bremmer and Devin T. Stewart	"China's State Capitalism Poses Ethical Challenges," GlobalPost, August 9, 2010. www.globalpost.com.
John Cassidy	"Enter the Dragon," *New Yorker*, December 13, 2010.
Economist	"Business in China: So Much for Capitalism," March 5, 2009.
Kevin A. Hassett	"Cronies Against Capitalism," *National Review*, March 24, 2008.
R. Jagannathan	"Big Government Means More Crony Capitalism," *Daily News & Analysis* (India), September 6, 2009.
Kishore Mahbubani	"Lessons for the West from Asian Capitalism," *Financial Times*, March 18, 2009.
Marian Tupy	"Africa Needs Free Market Economies," GlobalPost, February 6, 2010. www.globalpost.com.
William Watson	"William Watson: We're All Workers Now," *Financial Post*, December 2, 2010.

CHAPTER 2

Capitalism and the Global Financial Crisis

Unbridled Capitalism Is to Blame for the Worldwide Financial Crisis

Rowan Williams

In the following viewpoint, Rowan Williams argues that the global financial crisis was brought about by a lack of accountability in the market. He contends that the lack of regulation of capitalism allowed for wealth to be created based on fictional investments. Williams claims that the root of the problem is in believing in unregulated capitalism in a fundamentalist fashion rather than using the market to better the human community. Williams is the archbishop of Canterbury, the senior bishop and leader of the Church of England.

As you read, consider the following questions:

1. According to Williams, a particularly significant line is crossed when borrowing and lending become exclusively aimed at what goal?

2. The author gives what example of a practice that is banned because the social risk is unacceptably high?

3. Williams claims that the biggest challenge in the global financial crisis is recovering some sense of the connection between what two things?

Readers of [English novelist] Anthony Trollope will remember how thoughtless and greedy young men in the Victorian professions can be lured into ruin by accepting 'accommodation bills' from their shifty acquaintances. They make themselves liable for the debts of others; and only too late do they discover that they are trapped in a web of financial mechanics that forces them to pay hugely inflated sums for obligations or services they have had nothing to do with. Their own individual credit-worthiness, their own circumstances, even their own personal choices are all irrelevant: The debt has acquired a life of its own, quite independent of any real transaction they are involved in.

The Trading of Debts

A prescient student of Trollope would have seen that he is identifying an endemic feature of the world of borrowing and lending. A lender takes a calculated risk in offering the use of their money to someone else, and rates of interests express the recognition of this—and the rewards that may be secured for taking such a risk. But it is not too difficult to see how the notional gain involved here can be used as security against a further risk. And so the transaction moves further and further from the original transaction with its realistic assessment of levels of risk within the context of measurable standards of credit-worthiness. Any face-to-face element, any direct calculation of what and who is reasonably worth trusting (which assumes some common frame of reference), fades away. Like Trollope's hapless young clerics and feckless young landowners, individuals find that their own personal financial decisions and calculations have nothing to do with what is happening to their resources, in a process for which a debt is simply someone else's wholly disposable asset.

It is a sort of one-syllable nursery parable of what the last couple of weeks [in September 2008] have illustrated in the world of global finance and, of course, a reminder that what we have been witnessing is not just the product of a couple of irresponsible decades.

Trading the debts of others without accountability has been the motor of astronomical financial gain for many in recent years. Primitively, a loan transaction is something which enables someone to do what they might not otherwise be able to do—start a business, buy a house. Lenders identify what would count as reasonable security in the present and the future (present assets, future income) and decide accordingly.

But inevitably in complex and large-scale transactions, one person's debt becomes part of the security which the lender can offer to another potential customer. And a particularly significant line is crossed when the borrowing and lending are no longer to do with any kind of equipping someone to do something specific, but exclusively about enabling profit— sometimes, as with the now banned practice of short-selling, by effectively betting on the failure of a partner in the transaction.

Trading the debts of others without accountability has been the motor of astronomical financial gain for many in recent years.

The Speculative Market

This crisis exposes the element of basic unreality in the situation—the truth that almost unimaginable wealth has been generated by equally unimaginable levels of fiction, paper transactions with no concrete outcome beyond profit for traders. But while we are getting used to this sudden vision of the emperor's new clothes, there are one or two questions that, in government as in society at large, we at last have a chance to ask. Some of these are elementary and practical. Given that the risk to social stability overall in these processes has been shown to be so enormous, it is no use pretending that the financial world can maintain indefinitely the degree of exemption from scrutiny and regulation that it has got used to. To grant that without a basis of some common prosperity and stability, no speculative market can long survive is not to argue for rigid Soviet-style centralised direction. Insecure or failed states may provide a brief and golden opportunity for profiteering, but cannot sustain reliable institutions.

Without a background of social stability everyone will eventually suffer, including even the most resourceful, bold and ingenious of speculators. The question is not how to choose between total control and total deregulation, but how to identify the points and practices where social risk becomes unacceptably high. The banning of short-selling is an example of just such a judgment. Governments should not lose their nerve as they look to identify a few more targets.

Marx long ago observed the way in which unbridled capitalism became a kind of mythology, ascribing reality, power and agency to things that had no life in themselves.

Behind all this, though, is the deeper moral issue. We find ourselves talking about capital or the market almost as if they were individuals, with purposes and strategies, making choices, deliberating reasonably about how to achieve aims. We lose sight of the fact that they are things that we make. They are sets of practices, habits, agreements which have arisen through a mixture of choice and chance. Once we get used to speaking about any of them as if they had a life independent of actual human practices and relations, we fall into any number of destructive errors. We expect an abstraction called 'the market' to produce the common good or to regulate its potential excesses by a sort of natural innate prudence, like a physical organism or ecosystem. We appeal to 'business' to acquire public

"And what traditional American religion have you lost faith in, sir? / Capitalism," cartoon by Signe Wilkinson. Signe Wilkinson's Editorial Cartoon used with the permission of Signe Wilkinson, the Washington Post Writers group, and the Cartoonist Group. All rights reserved.

responsibility and moral vision. And so we lose sight of the fact that the market is not like a huge individual consciousness, that business is a practice carried on by persons who have to make decisions about priorities—not a machine governed by inexorable laws.

The Need to Avoid Fundamentalism

And this is part of the same mind-set that turns the specific, goal-related transactions of borrowing and lending into a process producing pseudo-things, paper assets—but pseudo-things that (when matters do not go well) cause real and crippling damage to actual persons and institutions. The biggest challenge in the present crisis is whether we can recover some sense of the connection between money and material reality—the production of specific things, the achievement of recognisably human goals that have something to do with a shared sense of what is good for the human community in the widest sense.

Of course business is not philanthropy, securing profit is a legitimate (if not a morally supreme) motivation for people, and the definition of what's good for the human community can be pretty widely drawn. It's true as well that, in some circumstances, loosening up a financial regime to allow for entrepreneurs and innovators to create wealth is necessary to draw whole populations out of poverty. But it is a sort of fundamentalism to say that this alone will secure stable and just outcomes everywhere.

Fundamentalism is a religious word, not inappropriate to the nature of the problem. [Revolutionary socialist Karl] Marx long ago observed the way in which unbridled capitalism became a kind of mythology, ascribing reality, power and agency to things that had no life in themselves; he was right about that, if about little else. And ascribing independent reality to what you have in fact made yourself is a perfect definition of what the Jewish and Christian scriptures call idolatry. What the present anxieties and disasters should be teaching us is to 'keep ourselves from idols', in the biblical phrase. The mythologies and abstractions, the pseudo-objects of much modern financial culture, are in urgent need of their own [atheist evolutionary biologist Richard] Dawkins or [columnist known for criticism of religion Christopher] Hitchens. We need to be reacquainted with our own capacity to choose—which means acquiring some skills in discerning true faith from false, and re-learning some of the inescapable face-to-face dimensions of human trust.

Entrepreneurial Capitalism Is Not to Blame for the Worldwide Financial Crisis

Leszek Balcerowicz

In the following viewpoint, Leszek Balcerowicz argues that despite what some critics have claimed, capitalism is not the cause of the global financial crisis. Instead, Balcerowicz suggests that the cause of the crisis is government interference with the market, rather than a pure market failure. Rather than attempting to reinvent market capitalism, Balcerowicz proposes that entrepreneurial capitalism be further released from the state. Balcerowicz, a Polish economist, is the former chairman of the National Bank of Poland and deputy prime minister of Poland.

As you read, consider the following questions:

1. Balcerowicz contends empirically minded people know that there is no good alternative to what market system?

2. According to the author, which three European countries developed the most extreme housing bubbles?

3. Balcerowicz warns that empirically dubious interpretations of the financial crisis that call for more statism could gain ground and cause damage in what two ways?

Only the rulers of Cuba, Venezuela, Iran and some ideologues in the West condemn capitalism. Empirically minded people know that there is no good alternative. However, capitalism takes many forms and evolves over time. The questions to ask, then, are "What capitalism?" and "Does the present crisis shed new light on this issue?"

The Need to Further Capitalism

The popular condemnations of "greed" in response to the crisis seem to me superficial. Economists are expected to explain human behaviour in terms of situational factors and not to compete with preachers and politicians. Equally unconvincing is the speculation about what [British economist] John Maynard Keynes would be saying were he alive.

As a preliminary step to a more productive analysis, let us recall that not long ago Japan Inc, the Rhineland model and other statist or corporatist varieties of capitalism were praised as a better alternative to the more market-oriented Anglo-Saxon variant of this system. Since then, based on solid empirical research, there has been a wave of deregulation of the product and labour markets, and the European Union [EU] has set itself the ambitious goals of the Lisbon Agenda [economic development plan].

The present crisis means we must take further measures to release entrepreneurial capitalism.

Faced with high structural unemployment, fiscal pressures and ageing societies, many Western economies have started to reform their overextended welfare states. China and India have accelerated their growth thanks to a reduction in the political control of their economies. Central and eastern European countries show that the more market reforms you accumulate, the faster is your longer-term growth. These and other initiatives have reduced the crippling statist bias and extended the role of markets and civil society. The present crisis means we must take further measures to release entrepreneurial capitalism, offsetting declines in gross domestic product caused by the financial crisis and the legacy of attempts to manage it, especially the hugely increased public debt.

A Problem with the Framework

But is the financial sector an exception? Can the crisis be interpreted as a pure market failure, which requires more public intervention? It is easy to agree on the facts—increased leverage and asset bubbles in many economies, as well as serious errors made at the top of huge financial conglomerates. Symptoms, however, should not be confused with causes, and it is with respect to the causes that there is serious disagreement.

The argument that we have witnessed a pure market failure fails the most elementary tests. Financial institutions and markets operate within the macroeconomic, regulatory and political framework created and maintained by public bodies, and it is empirically not difficult to point to the serious deficiencies of this framework that contributed to the present crisis.

There is scope for further analysis of the relative contributions of the US Federal Reserve's [Fed's] easy monetary policy in the early 2000s and the "savings glut" in some emerging economies. With a more restrictive Fed policy (and with more disciplined fiscal policy under George W. Bush, the former US president), there would have been initially slower growth but less increase in the savings glut later, a smaller buildup of financial imbalances and, as a result, less disruption to growth.

Excess liquidity encouraged the spread of powerful short-term incentives in the financial institutions. Fannie Mae and Freddie Mac [government-sponsored home mortgage lenders] were largely the tools of political intervention in the US housing market. Some financial regulations might have accelerated the spread of the originate-to-distribute model, which is

Government Intervention Is Responsible for the Crisis

The actual responsibility for our financial crisis lies precisely with massive government intervention, above all the intervention of the [US] Federal Reserve System in attempting to create capital out of thin air, in the belief that the mere creation of money and its being made available in the loan market is a substitute for capital created by producing and saving. This is a policy it has pursued since its founding, but with exceptional vigor since 2001, in its efforts to overcome the collapse of the stock market bubble whose creation it had previously inspired.

George Reisman, "The Myth That Laissez Faire Is Responsible for Our Financial Crisis," George Reisman's Blog on Economics, Politics, Society, and Culture, October 21, 2008. http://georgereismansblog.blogspot.com.

blamed for amplifying leverage and obscured the allocation of risks. Those EU economies that developed the most extreme housing bubbles—Britain, Ireland, Spain—stimulated demand for housing with tax breaks.

Analytically based lessons from the present crisis should focus on revisions of the macroeconomic and regulatory frameworks for financial markets that would reduce the risks of dangerous booms and the resulting busts. Policies that contribute to the emergence and growth of huge financial conglomerates—which, once in crisis, endanger the financial stability of whole countries—should be identified and eliminated.

Critics of Capitalism

These proposals have nothing to do with grandiose schemes for reinventing market capitalism. However, every crisis pro-

69

duces a shock to mass beliefs and thus may have policy consequences. In a democracy, the impact of economic crises is mediated by competing interpretations provided by intellectuals and politicians, and conveyed by the media. There is a risk that empirically dubious but emotionally attractive interpretations, which condemn markets and call for more statism, could gain ground. This would damage longer-term growth in the affected countries and could have serious geopolitical consequences if major Western economies, especially the US, already burdened by the legacy of the crisis, were to succumb while China continued its reforms.

[Economists Ludwig von] Mises, [Friedrich August] Hayek, [and Joseph] Schumpeter [and philosopher Robert] Nozick and other thinkers have noted that under democratic capitalism there are always influential intellectuals who condemn capitalism and call for the state to restrain the markets. Such an activity bears no risk and may be very rewarding. (This contrasts strongly with the consequences of criticising socialism while living under socialism.)

Dynamic, entrepreneurial capitalism has nowadays no serious external enemies; it can only be weakened from within.

Dynamic, entrepreneurial capitalism has nowadays no serious external enemies; it can only be weakened from within. This should be regarded as a call to action—for those who believe that individuals' prosperity and dignity are best ensured under limited government.

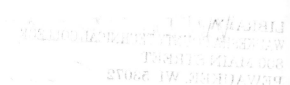

Capitalism Worldwide Is Threatened by US Government Response to the Financial Crisis

Gary S. Becker and Kevin Murphy

In the following viewpoint, Gary S. Becker and Kevin Murphy argue that although capitalism is partly responsible for the global financial crisis, capitalism over the last few decades has resulted in overall gains for the global economy. Becker and Murphy critique US government reactions to the financial crisis as making matters worse. They contend that the crisis will result in self-correction by the market and that government regulation that retreats from capitalist principles should be avoided. Becker and Murphy are professors of economics at the University of Chicago and fellows at the Hoover Institution.

As you read, consider the following questions:

1. Becker and Murphy claim that world real gross domestic product (GDP) grew by what percent from 1980 to 2007?

2. The authors suggest a scenario where President Barack Obama commits the United States to reduce consumer spending from 70 percent of GDP to what?

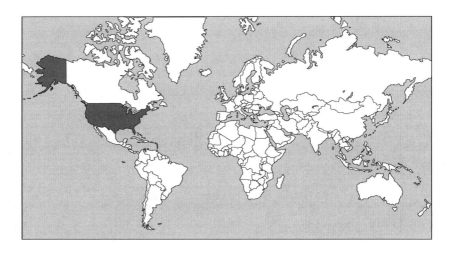

3. According to Becker and Murphy, the struggle for the soul of capitalism is a struggle between what two entities?

Capitalism has been wounded by the global recession, which unfortunately will get worse before it gets better. As governments continue to determine how many restrictions to place on markets, especially financial markets, the destruction of wealth from the recession should be placed in the context of the enormous creation of wealth and improved well-being during the past three decades. Financial and other reforms must not risk destroying the source of these gains in prosperity.

The Performance of Capitalism

Consider the following extraordinary statistics about the performance of the world economy since 1980. World real gross domestic product [GDP] grew by about 145 per cent from 1980 to 2007, or by an average of roughly 3.4 per cent a year. The so-called capitalist greed that motivated business people and ambitious workers helped hundreds of millions to climb out of grinding poverty. The role of capitalism in creating wealth is seen in the sharp rise in Chinese and Indian incomes after they introduced market-based reforms (China in the late 1970s and India in 1991). Global health, as measured by life expectancy at different ages, has also risen rapidly, especially in lower-income countries.

Of course, the performance of capitalism must include this recession and other recessions along with the glory decades. Even if the recession is entirely blamed on capitalism, and it deserves a good share of the blame, the recession-induced losses pale in comparison with the great accomplishments of prior decades. Suppose, for example, that the recession turns into a depression, where world GDP falls in 2008–10 by 10 per cent, a pessimistic assumption. Then the net growth in world GDP from 1980 to 2010 would amount to 120 per cent, or about 2.7 per cent a year over this 30-year period. This allowed real per capita incomes to rise by almost 40 per cent even though world population grew by roughly 1.6 per cent a year over the same period.

Even if the recession is entirely blamed on capitalism, . . . the recession-induced losses pale in comparison with the great accomplishments of prior decades.

Therefore, in devising reforms that aim to reduce the likelihood of future severe contractions, the accomplishments of capitalism should be appreciated. Governments should not so hamper markets that they are prevented from bringing rapid growth to the poor economies of Africa, Asia and elsewhere that have had limited participation in the global economy. New economic policies that try to speed up recovery should follow the first principle of medicine: do no harm. This runs counter to a common but mistaken view, even among many free-market proponents, that it is better to do something to try to help the economy than to do nothing. Most interventions, including random policies, by their very nature would hurt rather than help, in large part by adding to the uncertainty and risk that are already so prominent during this contraction.

Government Reactions to the Financial Crisis

Government reactions have demonstrated the danger that interventions designed to help can exacerbate the problem. Even though we had well-qualified policy makers, we have gone from error to error since August 2007.

The policies of the [George W.] Bush and [Barack] Obama administrations violate the "do no harm" principle. Interventions by the US Treasury in financial markets have added to the uncertainty and slowed market responses that would help stabilise and recapitalise the system. The government has overridden contracts and rewarded many of those whose poor decisions helped create the mess. It proposes to override even more contracts. As a result of the Treasury's actions, we face further distorted decision making as government ownership of big financial institutions threatens to substitute political agendas for business judgments in running these companies. While such dramatic measures may be expedient, they are likely to have serious adverse consequences.

The rush to "solve" the problems of the crisis has opened the door to government actions on many fronts.

These problems are symptomatic of three basic flaws in the current approach to the crisis. They are an overly broad diagnosis of the problem, a misconception that market failures are readily overcome by government solutions and a failure to focus on the long-run costs of current actions.

The rush to "solve" the problems of the crisis has opened the door to government actions on many fronts. Many of these have little or nothing to do with the crisis or its causes.

For example, the Obama administration has proposed sweeping changes to labour market policies to foster unionisation and a more centralised setting of wages, even though the relative freedom of US labour markets in no way contributed to the crisis and would help to keep it short. Similarly, the backlash against capitalism and "greed" has been used to justify more antitrust scrutiny, greater regulation of a range of markets, and an expansion of price controls for health care and pharmaceuticals. The crisis has led to a bailout of the US car industry and a government role in how it will be run. Even one of the most discredited ideas, protectionism, has gained support under the guise of stimulating the economy. Such policies would be a mistake. They make no more sense today than they did a few years ago and could take a long time to reverse.

The Counterproductive US Government Actions

The failure of financial innovations such as securities backed by subprime mortgages, problems caused by risk models that ignored the potential for steep falls in house prices and the overload of systemic risk represent clear market failures, although innovations in finance also contributed to the global boom over the past three decades.

The people who made mistakes lost, and many lost big. Institutions that made bad loans and investments had large declines in their wealth, while investors that funded these institutions without proper scrutiny have seen their wealth cut in half or much more. Households that overextended themselves have also been badly hurt.

Given the losses, actors in these markets have a strong incentive to correct their mistakes the next time. In this respect, many government actions have been counterproductive, shielding actors from the consequences of their actions and preventing private sector adjustments. The uncertainty from

A Threat to American Capitalism

The economic crisis of the past year [2008–09], centered as it has been in the financial sector that lies at the heart of American capitalism, is bound to leave some lasting marks. Financial regulation, the role of large banks, and the relationships between the government and key players in the market will never be the same.

More important, however, are the ways in which public attitudes about our system might change. The nature of the crisis, and of the government's response, now threaten to undermine the public's sense of the fairness, justice, and legitimacy of democratic capitalism. By allowing the conditions that made the crisis possible (particularly the concentration of power in a few large institutions), and by responding to the crisis as we have (especially with massive government bailouts of banks and large corporations), the United States today risks moving in the direction of European corporatism and the crony capitalism of more statist regimes. This, in turn, endangers America's unique brand of capitalism, which has thus far avoided becoming associated in the public mind with entrenched corruption, and has therefore kept this country relatively free of populist anti-capitalist sentiment.

Luigi Zingales, "Capitalism After the Crisis,"
National Affairs, *Fall 2009.*

muddled Treasury policy on bank capital and ownership structure, the willingness of the government to change mortgage and debt contracts unilaterally and the uncertain nature of future regulation and subsidies help prevent greater private recapitalisation. Rather than solving problems, such policies tend to prolong them.

The US stimulus bill falls into the same category. This package is partly based on the belief that government spending is required to stimulate the economy because private spending would be insufficient. The focus on government solutions is particularly disappointing given its poor record in dealing with crises in the US and many other countries, such as the aftermath of Hurricane Katrina and failure effectively to prosecute the war in Iraq.

The claim that the crisis was due to insufficient regulation is also unconvincing. For example, commercial banks have been more regulated than most other financial institutions, yet they performed no better, and in many ways worse. Regulators got caught up in the same bubble mentality as investors and failed to use the regulatory authority available to them.

We hope our leaders do not deviate far from a market-oriented global economic system.

The Danger of a Retreat from Capitalism

Output, employment and earnings have all been hit by the crisis and will get worse before they get better. Nevertheless, even big downturns represent pauses in long-run progress if we keep the engines of long-term growth in place. This growth depends on investment in human and physical capital and the production of new knowledge. That requires a stable economic environment. Uncertainty about the scope of regulation is likely to have the unintended consequence of making those investments more risky.

The Great Depression induced a massive worldwide retreat from capitalism, and an embrace of socialism and communism that continued into the 1960s. It also fostered a belief that the future lay in government management of the economy, not in freer markets. The result was generally slow growth during those decades in most of the undeveloped world, including China, the Soviet bloc nations, India and Africa.

Partly owing to the collapse of the housing and stock markets, hostility to business people and capitalism has grown sharply again. Yet a world that is mainly capitalistic is the "only game in town" that can deliver further large increases in wealth and health to poor as well as rich nations. We hope our leaders do not deviate far from a market-oriented global economic system. To do so would risk damaging a system that has served us well for 30 years.

The Crisis of Capitalism Requires That the United States Move Away from Consumerism

Benjamin R. Barber

In the following viewpoint, Benjamin R. Barber argues that the global financial crisis makes obvious the need for a fundamental change in attitudes and behavior toward the role of the market in society. Barber claims that for too long consumerism has been prized above all else and that it is time for a fundamental change, where capitalism serves our needs instead of fabricating further wants. Barber is Walt Whitman Professor Emeritus at Rutgers University, a distinguished senior fellow at Demos, and author of Consumed: How Markets Corrupt Children, Infantilize Adults, and Swallow Citizens Whole.

As you read, consider the following questions:

1. What comment by George Soros does Barber quote?
2. The author contends that reform should encourage people to do what rather than spend?
3. According to the author, what is the struggle for the soul of capitalism?

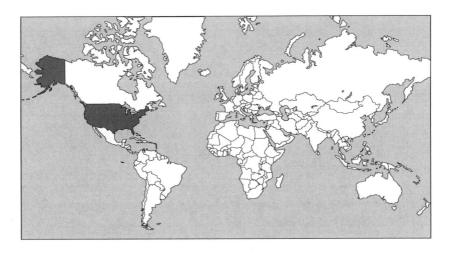

As America, recession mired, enters the hope-inspired age of Barack Obama, a silent but fateful struggle for the soul of capitalism is being waged. Can the market system finally be made to serve us? Or will we continue to serve it? George W. Bush argued that the crisis is "not a failure of the free-market system, and the answer is not to try to reinvent that system." But while it is going too far to declare that capitalism is dead, [businessman and philanthropist] George Soros is right when he says that "there is something fundamentally wrong" with the market theory that stands behind the global economy, a "defect" that is "inherent in the system."

The Need for a Wholesale Rethinking

The issue is not the death of capitalism but what kind of capitalism—standing in which relationship to culture, to democracy and to life? President Obama's Rubinite economic team seems designed to reassure rather than innovate, its members set to fix what they broke. But even if they succeed, will they do more than merely restore capitalism to the *status quo ante* [the way things were before], resurrecting all the defects that led to the current debacle?

Being economists, even the progressive critics missing from the Obama economic team continue to think inside the economic box. Yes, bankers and politicians agree that there must be more regulatory oversight, a greater government equity stake in bailouts and some considerable warming of the frozen credit pump. A very large stimulus package with a welcome focus on the environment, alternative energy, infrastructure and job creation is in the offing—a good thing indeed.

But it is hard to discern any movement toward a wholesale rethinking of the dominant role of the market in our society. No one is questioning the impulse to rehabilitate the consumer market as the driver of American commerce. Or to keep commerce as the foundation of American public and private life, even at the cost of rendering other cherished American values—like pluralism, the life of the spirit and the pursuit of (nonmaterial) happiness—subordinate to it.

Economists and politicians across the spectrum continue to insist that the challenge lies in revving up inert demand. For in an economy that has become dependent on consumerism to the tune of 70 percent of GDP [gross domestic product], shoppers who won't shop and consumers who don't consume spell disaster. Yet it is precisely in confronting the paradox of consumerism that the struggle for capitalism's soul needs to be waged.

It is hard to discern any movement toward a wholesale rethinking of the dominant role of the market in our society.

A Revolution in Spirit

The crisis in global capitalism demands a revolution in spirit—fundamental change in attitudes and behavior. Reform cannot merely rush parents and kids back into the mall; it must encourage them to shop less, to save rather than spend. If there's to be a federal lottery, the Obama administration should use it as an incentive for saving, a free ticket, say, for every ten bucks banked. Penalize carbon use by taxing gas so that it's $4 a gallon regardless of market price, curbing gas guzzlers and promoting efficient public transportation. And how about policies that give producers incentives to target real needs, even where the needy are short of cash, rather than to manufacture faux needs for the wealthy just because they've got the cash?

Or better yet, take in earnest that insincere MasterCard ad, and consider all the things money can't buy (most things!). Change some habits and restore the balance between body and spirit. Refashion the cultural ethos by taking culture seriously. The arts play a large role in fostering the noncommercial aspects of society. It's time, finally, for a cabinet-level arts and humanities post to foster creative thinking within government as well as throughout the country. Time for serious federal arts education money to teach the young the joys and powers of imagination, creativity and culture, as doers and spectators rather than consumers.

Recreation and physical activity are also public goods not dependent on private purchase. They call for parks and biking paths rather than multiplexes and malls. Speaking of the multiplex, why has the new communications technology been left almost entirely to commerce? Its architecture is democratic, and its networking potential is deeply social. Yet for the most part, it has been put to private and commercial rather than educational and cultural uses. Its democratic and artistic possibilities need to be elaborated, even subsidized.

Transforming the Consumerist Ethos

Of course, much of what is required cannot be leveraged by government policy alone, or by a stimulus package and new regulations over the securities and banking markets. A cultural ethos is at stake. For far too long our primary institutions—

from education and advertising to politics and entertainment—have prized consumerism above everything else, even at the price of infantilizing society. If spirit is to have a chance, they must join the revolution.

The costs of such a transformation will undoubtedly be steep, since they are likely to prolong the recession. Capitalists may be required to take risks they prefer to socialize (i.e., make taxpayers shoulder them). They will be asked to create new markets rather than exploit and abuse old ones; to simultaneously jump-start investments and inventions that create jobs and help generate those new consumers who will buy the useful and necessary things capitalists make once they start addressing real needs (try purifying tainted water in the Third World rather than bottling tap water in the First!).

For far too long our primary institutions—from education and advertising to politics and entertainment—have prized consumerism above everything else.

The good news is, people are already spending less, earning before buying (using those old-fashioned layaway plans) and feeling relieved at the shopping quasi-moratorium. Suddenly debit cards are the preferred plastic. Parental "gatekeepers" are rebelling against marketers who treat their 4-year-olds as consumers-to-be. Adults are questioning brand identities and the infantilization of their tastes. They are out in front of the politicians, who still seem addicted to credit as a cure-all for the economic crisis.

The Need for Fundamental Change

And Barack Obama? We elected a president committed in principle to deep change. Rather than try to back out of the mess we are in, why not find a way forward? What if Obama committed the United States to reducing consumer spending from 70 percent of GDP to 50 percent over the next ten years, bringing it to roughly where Germany's GDP is today [in early 2009]? The Germans have a commensurate standard of living and considerably greater equality. Imagine all the things we could do without having to shop: play and pray, create and relate, read and walk, listen and procreate—make art, make friends, make homes, make love.

Sound too soft? Too idealistic? If we are to survive the collapse of the unsustainable consumer capitalism that has possessed our body politic over the past three decades, idealism must become the new realism. For if the contest is between the material body defined by solipsistic acquisitiveness and the human spirit defined by imagination and compassion, then a purely technical economic response is what will be too soft, promising little more than a restoration of that shopaholic hell of hyper-consumerism that occasioned the current disaster.

The convergence of Obama's election and the collapse of the global credit economy marks a moment when radical change is possible.

There are epic moments in history, often catalyzed by catastrophe, that permit fundamental cultural change. The Civil War not only brought an end to slavery but knit together a wounded country, opened the West and spurred capitalist investment in ways that created the modern American nation. The Great Depression legitimized a radical expansion of democratic interventionism; but more important, it made Americans aware of how crucial equality and social justice (buried in capitalism's first century) were to America's survival as a democracy.

Today we find ourselves in another such seminal moment. Will we use it to rethink the meaning of capitalism and the relationship between our material bodies and the spirited psyches they are meant to serve? Between the commodity fetishism and single-minded commercialism that we have allowed to dominate us, and the pluralism, heterogeneity and spiritedness that constitute our professed national character?

A Moment When Radical Change Is Possible

President Obama certainly inspired many young people to think beyond themselves—beyond careerism and mindless consumerism. But our tendency is to leave the "higher" things to high-minded rhetoric and devote policy to the material. Getting people to understand that happiness cannot be bought, and that consumerism wears out not only the sole and the wallet but the will and the soul—that capitalism cannot survive long-term on credit and consumerism—demands programs and people, not just talk.

The convergence of Obama's election and the collapse of the global credit economy marks a moment when radical change is possible. But we will need the new president's leadership to turn the economic disaster into a cultural and democratic opportunity: to make service as important as selfishness (what about a national service program, universal and mandatory, linked to education?); to render community no less valid than individualism (lost social capital can be recreated through support for civil society); to make the needs of the spirit as worthy of respect as those of the body (assist the arts and don't chase religion out of the public square just because we want it out of City Hall); to make equality as important as individual opportunity ("equal opportunity" talk has become a way to avoid confronting deep structural inequality); to make prudence and modesty values no less commendable than speculation and hubris (saving is not just good economic policy; it's a beneficent frame of mind). Such values are neither conservative nor liberal but are at once cosmopolitan and deeply American. Their restoration could inaugurate a quiet revolution.

The struggle for the soul of capitalism is, then, a struggle between the nation's economic body and its civic soul: a struggle to put capitalism in its proper place, where it serves our nature and needs rather than manipulating and fabricating whims and wants. Saving capitalism means bringing it into harmony with spirit—with prudence, pluralism and those "things of the public" (*res publica*) that define our civic souls. A revolution of the spirit.

Is the new president up to it? Are we?

Australia Should Respond to the Financial Crisis by Rejecting Extreme Capitalism

Kevin Rudd

In the following viewpoint, Kevin Rudd argues that extreme capitalism, backed by a neoliberal ideology, caused the global financial crisis. He claims that the failure of neoliberalism shows that government does need to regulate the financial markets. Rudd contends that in Australia, the social democrats have long insisted on the central role of the state in regulating the market, and now they can help rebuild confidence by rejecting the tenets of extreme capitalism. Rudd is the former leader of Australia's Labor Party, serving as prime minister from 2007 to 2010, and is currently the minister for foreign affairs.

As you read, consider the following questions:

1. Rudd claims that the global financial crisis has called into question what orthodoxy of the past 30 years?

2. The author contends that neoliberalism, and the free-market fundamentalism it has produced, has been revealed as what?

3. Social democrats, according to Rudd, have an advantage over neoliberals of taking a consistent position of what?

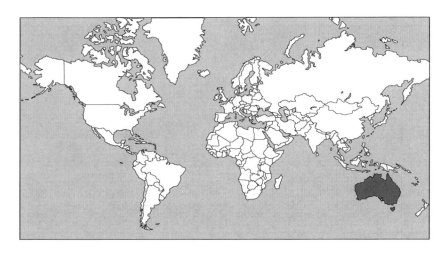

From time to time in human history there occur events of a truly seismic significance, events that mark a turning point between one epoch and the next, when one orthodoxy is overthrown and another takes its place. The significance of these events is rarely apparent as they unfold: It becomes clear only in retrospect, when observed from the commanding heights of history. By such time it is often too late to act to shape the course of such events and their effects on the day-to-day working lives of men and women and the families they support.

There is a sense that we are now living through just such a time: barely a decade into the new millennium, barely 20 years since the end of the Cold War [a period of tension between the United States and the Soviet Union in the second half of the 20th century] and barely 30 years since the triumph of neoliberalism—that particular brand of free-market fundamentalism, extreme capitalism and excessive greed which became the economic orthodoxy of our time.

The Global Financial Crisis

The agent for this change is what we now call the global financial crisis. In the space of just 18 months, this crisis has become one of the greatest assaults on global economic stability to have occurred in three-quarters of a century. As others have written, it "reflects the greatest regulatory failure in modern history". It is not simply a crisis facing the world's largest private financial institutions—systemically serious as that is in its own right. It is more than a crisis in credit markets, debt markets, derivatives markets, property markets and equity markets—notwithstanding the importance of each of these.

This is a crisis spreading across a broad front: It is a financial crisis which has become a general economic crisis; which is becoming an employment crisis; and which has in many countries produced a social crisis and in turn a political crisis. Indeed, accounts are already beginning to emerge of the long-term geopolitical implications of the implosion on Wall Street—its impact on the future strategic leverage of the West in general and the United States in particular.

The international challenge for social democrats is to save capitalism from itself: to recognise the great strengths of open, competitive markets while rejecting the extreme capitalism and unrestrained greed.

The global financial crisis has demonstrated already that it is no respecter of persons, nor of particular industries, nor of national boundaries. It is a crisis which is simultaneously individual, national and global. It is a crisis of both the developed and the developing world. It is a crisis which is at once institutional, intellectual and ideological. It has called into question the prevailing neoliberal economic orthodoxy of the past 30 years—the orthodoxy that has underpinned the national and global regulatory frameworks that have so spectacularly failed to prevent the economic mayhem which has now been visited upon us.

Not for the first time in history, the international challenge for social democrats is to save capitalism from itself: to recognise the great strengths of open, competitive markets while rejecting the extreme capitalism and unrestrained greed that have perverted so much of the global financial system in recent times. . . .

The Ideology That Caused the Crisis

[Businessman and philanthropist] George Soros has said that "the salient feature of the current financial crisis is that it was not caused by some external shock . . . the crisis was generated by the system itself". Soros is right. The current crisis is the culmination of a 30-year domination of economic policy by a free-market ideology that has been variously called neoliberalism, economic liberalism, economic fundamentalism, Thatcherism [the political style of conservative British prime minister Margaret Thatcher], or the Washington Consensus [neoliberal policies]. The central thrust of this ideology has been that government activity should be constrained, and ultimately replaced, by market forces.

In the past year [2008–2009], we have seen how unchecked market forces have brought capitalism to the precipice. The banking systems of the Western world have come close to collapse. Almost overnight, policy makers and economists have torn up the neoliberal playbook and governments have made unprecedented and extraordinary interventions to stop the panic and bring the global financial system back from the brink.

Even the great neoliberal ideological standard-bearer, the long-serving chairman of the US Federal Reserve Alan Greenspan, recently conceded in testimony before Congress that his ideological viewpoint was flawed, and that the "whole intellectual edifice" of modern risk management had collapsed. Henry Waxman, the chairman of the congressional Committee on Oversight and Government Reform, questioned Greenspan further: "In other words, you found that your view of the world, your ideology, was not right; it was not working?" Greenspan replied, "Absolutely, precisely." This *mea culpa* [acknowledgement of error] by the man once called 'the Maestro' has reverberated around the world.

To understand the failure of neoliberalism, it is necessary to consider its central elements. The ideology of the unrestrained free market, discredited by the Great Depression, re-emerged in the 1970s amid a widespread belief that the prevailing economic woes of high inflation and low growth were exclusively the result of excessive government intervention in the market. In the '80s, the [Ronald] Reagan and Thatcher governments gave political voice to this neoliberal movement of anti-tax, anti-regulation, anti-government conservatives.

The Core Belief of Neoliberalism

Neoliberal policy prescriptions flow from the core theoretical belief in the superiority of unregulated markets—particularly unregulated financial markets. These claims ultimately rest on the "efficient-markets hypothesis", which, in its strongest form, claims that financial market prices, like stock market prices, incorporate all available information, and therefore represent the best possible estimate of asset prices. It follows, therefore, that if markets are fully efficient and prices fully informed, there is no reason to believe that asset-price bubbles are probable; and if these do occur, markets will self-correct; and that there is therefore no justification for government intervention to stop them occurring. Indeed, in the neoliberal view, deviations from market efficiency must be attributable to external causes. Bubbles and other disruptions are caused by governments and other "imperfections", not by markets themselves. This theory justifies the belief that individual self-interest should be given free rein and that the income distribution generated by markets should be regarded as natural and inherently just. In the neoliberal view, markets are spontaneous and self-regulating products of civil society, while governments are alien and coercive intruders. . . .

The advocates of neoliberalism have sought, wherever possible, to dismantle all aspects of the social-democratic state. The idea of social solidarity, reflected in the collective provision of social goods, is dismissed as statist nonsense. In the face of vigorous resistance to cuts in public services, the neoliberal political project has followed a strategy of "starving the beast", cutting taxes in order to strangle the capacity of the government to invest in education, health and economic infrastructure. The end point: to provide maximal space in the economy for private markets.

Neoliberal policy prescriptions flow from the core theoretical belief in the superiority of unregulated markets— particularly unregulated financial markets.

Neoliberalism progressively became the economic orthodoxy. It was reflected in wave after wave of tax cuts. Governments bragged about their success in reducing measured levels of debt, while refusing to acknowledge the long-term economic cost of non-investment in education, skills and training (which increase productivity), and repudiating an appropriate role for public debt in financing investment in the infrastructure that underpins long-term economic growth. Neoliberals have also exhibited a passionate commitment to the total deregulation of the labour market. Labour is routinely regarded by neoliberals as no different from any other economic commodity. In the ideal neoliberal system, labour-market protections should be restricted to physical safety rather than appropriate remuneration or minimum negotiation standards. Again, contract law, rather than any wider concept of a social contract, should prevail. Neoliberals in government also become notoriously reluctant to identify and respond to instances of market failure. . . .

The Failure of Neoliberalism

Despite three crises in a decade, despite the clear warnings that came with them and after them, the neoliberals were so convinced of the ideological righteousness of their cause, and so blinded by their unquestioning belief that markets were inherently self-correcting, that they refused even to recognise the severity of the problems that emerged. The problems did not fit the model, so the evidence was simply discarded. Hardline neoliberals were not interested, because they knew in their hearts they were right.

The time has come, off the back of the current crisis, to proclaim that the great neoliberal experiment of the past 30 years has failed, that the emperor has no clothes. Neoliberalism, and the free-market fundamentalism it has produced, has been revealed as little more than personal greed dressed up as an economic philosophy. And, ironically, it now falls to social democracy to prevent liberal capitalism from cannibalising itself.

With the demise of neoliberalism, the role of the state has once more been recognised as fundamental. The state has been the primary actor in responding to three clear areas of the current crisis: in rescuing the private financial system from collapse; in providing direct stimulus to the real economy because of the collapse in private demand; and in the design of a national and global regulatory regime in which government has ultimate responsibility to determine and enforce the rules of the system.

The challenge for social democrats today is to recast the role of the state and its associated political economy of social democracy as a comprehensive philosophical framework for the future—tempered both for times of crisis and for times of prosperity. In doing so, social democrats will draw in part on a long-standing Keynesian tradition. Social democrats will also need to reach beyond [British economist John Maynard]

Keynes, given some of the new realities we face some 70 years after the publication of Keynes's *The General Theory [of Employment, Interest and Money]*.

The Middle Way

Long before the term 'Third Way' was popularised in the policy literature of the 1990s, social democrats viewed themselves as presenting a political economy of the middle way, which rejected both state socialism and free-market fundamentalism. Instead, social democrats maintain robust support for the market economy but posit that markets can only work in a mixed economy, with a role for the state as regulator and as a funder and provider of public goods. Transparency and competitive neutrality, ensured by a regime of competition and consumer-protection law, are essential.

> *Neoliberalism, and the free-market fundamentalism it has produced, has been revealed as little more than personal greed dressed up as an economic philosophy.*

Social justice is also viewed as an essential component of the social-democratic project. The social-democratic pursuit of social justice is founded on a belief in the self-evident value of equality, rather than, for example, an exclusively utilitarian argument that a particular investment in education is justified because it yields increases in productivity growth (although, happily, from the point of view of modern social democrats, both things happen to be true). Expressed more broadly, the pursuit of social justice is founded on the argument that all human beings have an intrinsic right to human dignity, equality of opportunity and the ability to lead a fulfilling life. In a similar vein, [Indian economist] Amartya Sen writes of freedom as the means to achieve economic stability and growth, but also as an end in itself. Accordingly, government has a clear role in the provision of such public goods as universal education, health, unemployment insurance, disabilities insurance and retirement income. This contrasts with the Hayekian view [named after Friedrich August Hayek] that a person's worth should primarily, and unsentimentally, be determined by the market.

Social-democratic governments face the continuing challenge of harnessing the power of the market to increase innovation, investment and productivity growth—while combining this with an effective regulatory framework which manages risk, corrects market failures, funds and provides public goods, and pursues social equity. Examples of such a government are the Australian Labor governments of Bob Hawke and Paul Keating during the 1980s and early '90s. Hawke and Keating pursued an ambitious and unapologetic program of economic modernisation. Their reforms internationalised the Australian economy, removed protectionist barriers and opened it up to greater competition. They were able dramatically to improve the productivity of the Australian private economy, while simultaneously expanding the role of the state in the provision of equity-enhancing public services in health and education.

A Central Role for Government

In the current crisis, social democrats therefore have the great advantage of a consistent position on the central role of the state—in contrast to neoliberals, who now find themselves tied in ideological knots, in being forced to rely on the state they fundamentally despise to save financial markets from collapse. This enables social-democratic governments to undertake such current practical tasks as credit-market regulation, intervention, and demand-side stimulus in the economy. The uncomfortable truth for neoliberals is that they have not been able to turn to non-state actors or non-state mechanisms to defray risk and restore confidence, rebuild balance sheets and unlock global capital flows. This is only possible through the agency of the state. . . .

The contrast between the competing political traditions within Australia on the role of governments and the market is clear. Labor, in the international tradition of social democracy, consistently argues for a central role for government in the regulation of markets and the provision of public goods.

Consistent with this tradition, the Labor government has acted decisively through state action to maintain the stability of the Australian financial systems in the face of the economic crisis. The government acted in October [2008] to guarantee all deposits. To support intra-bank lending by the Australian majors, it intervened to provide a facility for guaranteeing wholesale funding of financial institutions. To encourage liquidity, the government legislated to increase by $25 billion the maximum value of government bonds that can be issued at any one time. It also initiated a program to purchase residential mortgage-backed securities. To protect financial institutions from predatory speculators, a temporary ban on short-selling was introduced. Labor has also acted to help the real economy, to stimulate economic activity by investing in targeted job creation; in the reform of services in health, education, disabilities and homelessness; and in roads, rail, ports and other critical infrastructure. All through decisive state action.

> *Labor, in the international tradition of social democracy, consistently argues for a central role for government in the regulation of markets and the provision of public goods.*

The liberals, embracing the neoliberal tradition of anti-regulation, seek to reduce the agency of the state in private markets as much as possible. The distinction is reflected in the previous prime minister's statements that "competitive capitalism within free markets remains the most effective economic paradigm, both domestically and internationally"; that "the

right responses will be grounded in free-market orthodoxies";
and that "we should avoid the resort to re-regulation." This
ideology has not served Australia well in preparing for the
current crisis.

The New Ideology

To respond effectively to the global financial crisis in the future requires the resolution of profound questions from the
past, principal among which is: What caused such a crisis to
result in widespread economic and social devastation? The
magnitude of the crisis and its impact across the world means
that minor tweakings of long-established orthodoxies will not
do. Two unassailable truths have already been established: that
financial markets are not always self-correcting or self-
regulating, and that government (nationally and
internationally) can never abdicate responsibility for maintaining economic stability. These two truths in themselves destroy neoliberalism's claims to any continuing ideological legitimacy, because they remove the foundations on which the
entire neoliberal system is constructed. . . .

For social democrats, it is critical that we get it right—not
just to save the system of open markets from self-destruction,
but also to rebuild confidence in properly regulated markets,
so as to prevent extreme reactions from the Far Left or the Far
Right taking hold. Social democrats must also get it right because the stakes are so high: there are the economic and social
costs of long-term unemployment; poverty once again expanding its grim reach across the developing world; and the
impact on long-term power structures within the existing international political and strategic order. Success is not op-
tional. Too much now rides on our ability to prevail.

I believe that social democrats can chart an effective course
that will see us through this crisis, and one that is also capable
of building a fairer and more resilient order for the long term.
This can only be achieved through the creative agency of gov-

ernment—and through governments acting together. How could it possibly now be argued that the minimalist state of which the neoliberals have dreamt could somehow be of sufficient potency to respond to the maximalist challenge we have been left in the wake of this most spectacular failure of the entire neoliberal orthodoxy? Government is not the intrinsic evil that neoliberals have argued it is. Government, properly constituted and properly directed, is for the common good, embracing both individual freedom and fairness, a project designed for the many, not just the few.

The Impact of the Crisis on the Developing World Shows the Failure of Global Capitalism

Jayati Ghosh

In the following viewpoint, Jayati Ghosh argues that the recent boom and bust of global capitalism has increased inequalities within the countries of the developing world, as well as between the developing world and developed world. She argues that global capitalism has never worked well for developing countries and the crisis made things worse. Ghosh calls for a new model involving financial regulation and more sustainable production and consumption. Ghosh is professor of economics at Jawaharlal Nehru University in New Delhi, India, and the executive secretary of International Development Economics Associates (IDEAS).

As you read, consider the following questions:

1. What two countries does Ghosh claim were widely seen as delinked from the North prior to 2009?

2. The author contends that investment in the North by the South in the years leading up to the financial crisis shattered what notion?

3. Ghosh predicts that within two decades, what fraction of the population in developing countries will live in urban areas?

Developing countries have never been immune to the storms that rage in financial markets in industrial countries, or to the impact of recession in the core of capitalism, but the recent period is somewhat unusual in the history of global capitalism. For most of the past century, business cycles in advanced economies were not reflected so sharply in simultaneous movements in developing countries, or were generally confined to only a small set of countries. But the recent economic trends have been marked by significant synchronicity of movement across the different regions of the world economy. The difficulties have been particularly extreme in certain regions, such as eastern and central Europe, which were until recently the 'beneficiaries' of large amounts of inflows of speculative finance capital; these have created domestic bubbles not unlike the larger and more dramatic one in the US. But all regions of the developing world have been affected to varying degrees by this particular crisis.

The Global Crisis in the Developing World

This sharp and almost immediate transmission of recessionary tendencies is strongly related to the various forms of economic integration that have been generally induced by policy changes across the world during the years of globalisation, in both developed and developing countries. As a result, there are now several transmission mechanisms operating to spread the crisis, including exports of goods and services; capital flows; patterns of migration and remittances; and sharp changes in world trade prices of important essential items like oil and food.

Among developing countries, China and India were widely seen to have 'decoupled' or delinked from the North, and as having their own autonomous growth trajectories. It was even believed that this could make them an alternative growth pole in the world economy. But the past year [2009–2010] has belied such perceptions, as the first negative impulses from finance and trade caused even China and India to show similar trends of sharply declining growth rates of GDP [gross domestic product]. The relatively rapid current recovery of the Chinese economy, which reflects the impact of the fiscal stimulus and other recovery measures such as massive credit expansion, conceals the continued and fundamental dependence of the current Chinese accumulation strategy on Northern markets.

What has made the impact of the crisis worse in many developing countries is that it occurred after (and because of) an extremely imbalanced boom that was based upon, and intensified, inequalities.

What has made the impact of the crisis worse in many developing countries is that it occurred after (and because of) an extremely unbalanced boom that was based upon, and intensified, inequalities, with the poor of the world subsidising the rich, both nationally and internationally. The financial bubble in the US attracted savings from across the world, including from the poorest developing countries, so that for at least five years the South was transferring financial resources to the North. Developing country governments opened up their markets to trade and finance, gave up on monetary policy and pursued fiscally 'correct' deflationary policies that reduced public spending. This meant that development projects remained incomplete and citizens were deprived of the most essential socioeconomic rights, even in peripheral economies that were supposedly benefiting from the export boom.

Capital and Jobs in the Developing World

Despite popular perceptions, a net transfer of jobs from North to South did not take place during this period. In fact, industrial employment in the South barely increased during the past decade, even in the 'factory of the world' China. Instead, technological change in manufacturing and the new services meant that fewer workers could generate more output. While there have been significant changes in the forms of work, the recent capitalist boom was associated with hardly any net employment creation in the periphery. Old jobs in the South were lost or became precarious, and the majority of new jobs were fragile, insecure and low-paying, even in fast-growing China and India. One major shift has been the expansion of self-employment, typically in marketed but 'informal' activities, reflecting the absolute shortage of paid work, and the outsourcing of work to lower and lower levels. Women workers have been disproportionately involved in the lowest level of such activities, in home-based work. This has also meant that the risks of production have been typically passed on to the 'self-employed' workers at the bottom of the production chains that have emerged. Furthermore, the persistent agrarian crisis in the developing world damaged peasant livelihoods even as other forms of productive employment were not available. Across different national economies, profit shares of national income soared and wage shares declined sharply.

Almost all developing countries and formerly socialist economies adopted an export-led market-oriented accumulation model, which in turn was associated with suppressing wage costs and domestic consumption in order to remain internationally competitive and achieve growing shares of world markets. This led to the peculiar situation of rising savings rates but falling investment rates in many developing countries, and to the holding of international reserves that were then sought to be placed in safe assets abroad. This is why the boom that preceded the recession was associated with the global South subsidising the North: through cheaper exports of goods and services, through net capital flows from developing countries to the US in particular, through flows of cheap labour in the form of short-term migration.

An Increase in Global Inequality

In this boom, domestic demand tended to be profit-led, based on high and growing profit shares in the economy and significant increases in the income and consumption of newly globalised middle classes, and this led to bullish investment in certain non-tradeable sectors such as financial assets and real estate as well as in luxury goods and services. These forms of demand and investment enabled many Southern economies to keep growing even though agriculture was in crisis and employment was not expanding enough to sustain growth. The patterns of production and consumption that emerged meant that growth involved rapacious and ultimately destructive exploitation of nature and the environment. As is typical under capitalism, the costs and ecological constraints of such growth were already being felt among the regions and people of the world who gained the least from the overall expansion of incomes during the boom.

The five years preceding the crisis witnessed an unprecedented increase in gross private capital flows to developing countries. Remarkably, however, this was not accompanied by a net transfer of financial resources, because all developing regions chose to accumulate foreign exchange reserves rather than actually use the money. Thus, there was an even more unprecedented counterflow from South to North, in the form of central bank investments in the safe assets and sovereign wealth funds of developing countries—a process which completely shattered the notion (if any further proof were needed) that free capital markets generate net financial flows from rich to poor countries.

The current collapse in export markets has brought that process to a stop, but in any case such a strategy is unsustainable beyond a certain point, especially when a number of relatively large economies seek to use it at the same time. So not only was this a strategy that bred and increased global inequality; it also sowed the seeds of its own destruction by generating downward pressures on price because of increasing competition as well as protectionist responses in the core of international capitalism. . . .

It is evident that global capitalism is near a tipping point, and the model of development that drove recent capitalist expansion in the periphery is no longer possible.

A New Developmental Model

The ability of governments to undertake effective policy responses is conditioned by the extent to which they have been battered by the crisis in the first place. In particular, the extent of financial contagion and possible local financial crisis has depended on how far each country has gone along the road of financial liberalisation. Countries with large external debts and current account deficits have faced particular problems. Countries that have gone furthest in terms of deregulating their financial markets along the lines of the US have been the worst affected, and may well have full-blown financial crises of their own. By contrast, China, which has still kept most of the banking system under state control and has not allowed many of the financial 'innovations' that are responsible for the current mess in developed markets, is relatively safe. In addition, the countries that are most able to take effective measures to revive employment, control food prices and so on are those that are least dependent upon foreign resources.

The crisis points to the need for a new development model. It is evident that global capitalism is near a tipping point, and the model of development that drove recent capitalist expansion in the periphery is no longer possible. This is true at many different levels. First, in the near future the US will no longer continue to be the engine of world growth through increasing import demand. This means that countries that have relied on the US and the EU [European Union] as their primary export markets and important source of final demand must seek to redirect their exports to other countries, and most of all to redirect their economies towards more domestic demand. Even within capitalist developing economies, this requires a shift towards wage-led and domestic-demand-led growth. This in turn requires both direct redistributive strategies and public expenditure to provide more basic goods and services.

Second, even for minimally stable capitalism, it is now clear that there is no alternative to systematic state regulation and control of finance. Since private players will inevitably attempt to circumvent regulation, the core of the financial system banking must be protected, and this is only possible through social ownership. Therefore, some degree of socialisation of banking (and not just socialisation of the risks inherent in finance) is also inevitable. In developing countries this is all the more important in that it enables public control over the direction of credit, without which no country has yet industrialised.

Addressing Unsustainable Production and Consumption

Third, the ecological constraints on growth are appearing very rapidly, not only in terms of climate change but also because of the pollution, degradation and overexploitation of nature that has been a major aspect of past growth. Unsustainable patterns of production and consumption are now deeply entrenched in the richer countries and are aspired to in developing countries, even as many millions of citizens of the developing world still have poor or inadequate access to the most basic conditions of decent life. Basic changes in patterns of production and consumption are required, as well as reductions in inequalities in income and wealth.

These problems have been exacerbated by the single-minded focus in all developing economies on quantitative

The Hungry of the World

Food and economic crises put the number of hungry people over one billion in 2009

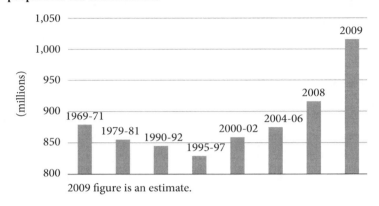

2009 figure is an estimate.

Most of the world's undernourished live in developing countries

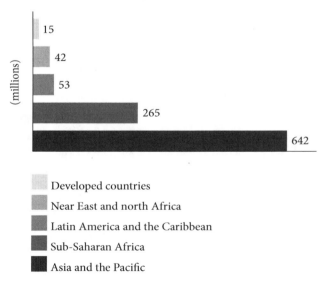

- Developed countries
- Near East and north Africa
- Latin America and the Caribbean
- Sub-Saharan Africa
- Asia and the Pacific

TAKEN FROM: "Hunger on the Rise," *Finance & Development*, March 2010.

GDP growth targets. These reflect the focus on increasing profits and continuously driving the process of accumulation, but they can be counterproductive from the point of view of meeting real human needs. For example, a chaotic, polluting and unpleasant system of privatised urban transport involving many private vehicles and over-congested roads actually generates more GDP than a safe, efficient and affordable system of public transport that reduces vehicular congestion and provides a pleasant living and working environment. So it is not enough to talk about 'cleaner, greener technologies' if they are going to produce goods that are based on the old and now discredited pattern of consumption. Instead, we must think creatively about such consumption itself, and work out which goods and services are more necessary and desirable for our societies.

Sixth, this cannot be left to market forces, since the international demonstration effect and the power of advertising will continue to create undesirable wants and unsustainable consumption and production. But public intervention in the market must not consist of knee-jerk responses to constantly changing short-term conditions. Instead, planning is absolutely essential—not in the sense of the detailed planning that destroyed the reputation of command regimes, but in terms of strategic thinking about the social requirements and goals for the future. Fiscal and monetary policies, as well as other forms of intervention, will have to be deployed in order to redirect consumption and production towards these social goals—to bring about shifts in socially created aspirations and material wants, and reorganise economic life to be less rapacious and more sustainable.

This is particularly important for quality of life in urban areas: The high rates of urbanisation in developing countries mean that even in many countries that are now dominantly rural, within two decades more than half the population will live in urban areas. Yet, because, in the developing world especially, we still do not plan for the future to make our cities pleasant or even livable for most residents, we tend to create urban monstrosities of congestion, inequality and insecurity.

Since state involvement in economic activity is now an imperative, we should be thinking of ways to make such involvement more democratic and accountable.

A New Economic Framework

Seventh, since state involvement in economic activity is now an imperative, we should be thinking of ways to make such involvement more democratic and accountable, within our countries and internationally. Large amounts of public money will be used for financial bailouts and to provide fiscal stimuli, and the ways in which this is done will have huge implications for distribution, access to resources, and living conditions of the ordinary people whose taxes will be paying for it. So it is essential that we design the global economic architecture to function more democratically. And it is even more important that states across the world, when formulating and implementing economic policies, are more open and responsive to the needs of the majority of their citizens.

Finally, we need an international economic framework that supports all these strategies, and this means more than just the control and regulation of capital flows to prevent them from destabilising them. The global institutions that form the organising framework for international trade, investment and production decisions also need to change, to become not just more democratic in structure, but more genuinely democratic and people-oriented in spirit, intent and functioning. Financing for development and conservation of global resources must become the top priorities of the global economic institutions, which means in turn that they cannot continue to base their approach on a completely discredited and unbalanced economic model.

Periodical and Internet Sources Bibliography

The following articles have been selected to supplement the diverse views presented in this chapter.

Roger C. Altman	"The Great Crash, 2008: A Geopolitical Setback for the West," *Foreign Affairs*, January/February 2009.
Jagdish Bhagwati	"Feeble Critiques: Capitalism's Petty Detractors," *World Affairs*, Fall 2009.
Terrence Corcoran	"Terence Corcoran: Capitalism's Comeback," *Financial Post*, January 7, 2011.
Steven Kates	"Reflections of a Neo-Liberal," *Quadrant*, April 2009.
Owen Matthews	"Out of Pocket," *Newsweek International*, November 10, 2008.
Edmund Phelps	"Uncertainty Bedevils the Best System," *Financial Times*, April 14, 2009.
Michael Schuman	"Why Government Intervention Won't Last," *Time*, November 25, 2008.
Amartya Sen	"Capitalism Beyond the Crisis," *New York Review of Books*, March 26, 2009.
Walter E. Williams	"Capitalism and the Financial Crisis," Town hall.com, November 5, 2008. http://townhall.com.
Martin Wolf	"This Crisis Is a Moment, but Is It a Defining One?" *Financial Times*, May 19, 2009.
Luigi Zingales	"Capitalism After the Crisis," *National Affairs*, Fall 2009.

GLOBALVIEWPOINTS

CHAPTER 3

Capitalism and Democracy

Capitalism Is Threatening Democracy Worldwide

Robert B. Reich

In the following viewpoint, Robert B. Reich argues that the line between capitalism and democracy has been blurred, with the assumption that they each create the other. Reich contends that capitalism has gained the upper hand around the world and is threatening the role of democracy. He concludes that it is necessary to understand the respective purposes of each in order keep capitalism from undermining democracy. Reich is Chancellor's Professor of Public Policy at the Goldman School of Public Policy at the University of California, Berkeley, and has served in three presidential administrations. He is the author of Supercapitalism: The Transformation of Business, Democracy, and Everyday Life.

As you read, consider the following questions:

1. According to Reich, what three countries have embraced capitalism but not democracy?

2. The author claims that in Japan, the share of Japanese households without savings increased by what factor between 1999 and 2005?

3. Reich contends that the only way for the citizen within to trump the consumer within is through what?

It was supposed to be a match made in heaven. Capitalism and democracy, we've long been told, are the twin ideological pillars capable of bringing unprecedented prosperity and freedom to the world. In recent decades, the duo has shared a common ascent. By almost any measure, global capitalism is triumphant. Most nations around the world are today part of a single, integrated, and turbocharged global market. Democracy has enjoyed a similar renaissance. Three decades ago, a third of the world's nations held free elections; today, nearly two-thirds do.

Capitalism and Democracy

Conventional wisdom holds that where either capitalism or democracy flourishes, the other must soon follow. Yet today, their fortunes are beginning to diverge. Capitalism, long sold as the yin to democracy's yang, is thriving, while democracy is struggling to keep up. China, poised to become the world's third largest capitalist nation this year [2007] after the United States and Japan, has embraced market freedom, but not political freedom. Many economically successful nations—from Russia to Mexico—are democracies in name only. They are encumbered by the same problems that have hobbled American democracy in recent years, allowing corporations and elites buoyed by runaway economic success to undermine the government's capacity to respond to citizens' concerns.

Of course, democracy means much more than the process of free and fair elections. It is a system for accomplishing what can only be achieved by citizens joining together to further the common good. But though free markets have brought unprecedented prosperity to many, they have been accompanied by widening inequalities of income and wealth, heightened job insecurity, and environmental hazards such as global warming. Democracy is designed to allow citizens to address these very issues in constructive ways. And yet a sense of political powerlessness is on the rise among citizens in Europe,

Japan, and the United States, even as consumers and investors feel more empowered. In short, no democratic nation is effectively coping with capitalism's negative side effects.

Capitalism, long sold as the yin to democracy's yang, is thriving, while democracy is struggling to keep up.

This fact is not, however, a failing of capitalism. As these two forces have spread around the world, we have blurred their responsibilities, to the detriment of our democratic duties. Capitalism's role is to increase the economic pie, nothing more. And while capitalism has become remarkably responsive to what people want as individual consumers, democracies have struggled to perform their own basic functions: to articulate and act upon the common good, and to help societies achieve both growth and equity. Democracy, at its best, enables citizens to debate collectively how the slices of the pie should be divided and to determine which rules apply to private goods and which to public goods. Today, those tasks are increasingly being left to the market. What is desperately needed is a clear delineation of the boundary between global capitalism and democracy—between the economic game, on the one hand, and how its rules are set, on the other. If the purpose of capitalism is to allow corporations to play the market as aggressively as possible, the challenge for citizens is to stop these economic entities from being the authors of the rules by which we live.

The Conflict Between Consumer and Citizen

Most people are of two minds: As consumers and investors, we want the bargains and high returns that the global economy provides. As citizens, we don't like many of the social consequences that flow from these transactions. We like to blame corporations for the ills that follow, but in truth we've made this compact with ourselves. After all, we know the roots of the great economic deals we're getting. They come from workers forced to settle for lower wages and benefits. They come from companies that shed their loyalties to communities and morph into global supply chains. They come from CEOs [chief executive officers] who take home exorbitant paychecks. And they come from industries that often wreak havoc on the environment.

Unfortunately, in the United States, the debate about economic change tends to occur between two extremist camps: those who want the market to rule unimpeded, and those who want to protect jobs and preserve communities as they are. Instead of finding ways to soften the blows of globalization, compensate the losers, or slow the pace of change, we go to battle. Consumers and investors nearly always win the day, but citizens lash out occasionally in symbolic fashion, by attempting to block a new trade agreement or protesting the sale of U.S. companies to foreign firms. It is a sign of the inner conflict Americans feel—between the consumer in us and the citizen in us—that the reactions are often so schizophrenic.

Such conflicting sentiments are hardly limited to the United States. The recent wave of corporate restructurings in Europe has shaken the continent's typical commitment to job security and social welfare. It's leaving Europeans at odds as to whether they prefer the private benefits of global capitalism in the face of increasing social costs at home and abroad. Take, for instance, the auto industry. In 2001, DaimlerChrysler faced mounting financial losses as European car buyers abandoned the company in favor of cheaper competitors. So, CEO Dieter Zetsche cut 26,000 jobs from his global workforce and closed six factories. Even profitable companies are feeling the pressure to become ever more efficient. In 2005, Deutsche Bank simultaneously announced an 87 percent increase in net profits and a plan to cut 6,400 jobs, nearly half of them in Germany and Britain. Twelve hundred of the jobs were then moved to low-wage nations. Today, European consumers and investors are doing better than ever, but job insecurity and inequality are rising, even in social democracies that were established to counter the injustices of the market. In the face of such change, Europe's democracies have shown themselves to be so paralyzed that the only way citizens routinely express opposition is through massive boycotts and strikes.

It is a sign of the inner conflict Americans feel—between the consumer in us and the citizen in us—that the reactions are often so schizophrenic.

Capitalism in Asia

In Japan, many companies have abandoned lifetime employment, cut workforces, and closed down unprofitable lines. Just months after Howard Stringer was named Sony's first non-Japanese CEO, he announced the company would trim 10,000 employees, about 7 percent of its workforce. Surely some Japanese consumers and investors benefit from such corporate downsizing: By 2006, the Japanese stock market had reached a 14-year high. But many Japanese workers have been left behind. A nation that once prided itself on being an "all middle-class society" is beginning to show sharp disparities in income and wealth. Between 1999 and 2005, the share of Japanese households without savings doubled, from 12 percent to 24 percent. And citizens there routinely express a sense of powerlessness. Like many free countries around the world, Japan is embracing global capitalism with a democracy too enfeebled to face the free market's many social penalties.

On the other end of the political spectrum sits China, which is surging toward capitalism without democracy at all. That's good news for people who invest in China, but the social consequences for the country's citizens are mounting. Income inequality has widened enormously. China's new business elites live in McMansions inside gated suburban communities and send their children to study overseas. At the same time, China's cities are bursting with peasants from the countryside who have sunk into urban poverty and unemployment. And those who are affected most have little political recourse to change the situation, beyond riots that are routinely put down by force.

But citizens living in democratic nations aren't similarly constrained. They have the ability to alter the rules of the game so that the cost to society need not be so great. And yet, we've increasingly left those responsibilities to the private sector—to the companies themselves and their squadrons of lobbyists and public relations experts—pretending as if some inherent morality or corporate good citizenship will compel them to look out for the greater good. But they have no responsibility to address inequality or protect the environment on their own. We forget that they are simply duty bound to protect the bottom line.

The Purpose of Capitalism

Why has capitalism succeeded while democracy has steadily weakened? Democracy has become enfeebled largely because companies, in intensifying competition for global consumers and investors, have invested ever greater sums in lobbying, public relations, and even bribes and kickbacks, seeking laws that give them a competitive advantage over their rivals. The result is an arms race for political influence that is drowning out the voices of average citizens. In the United States, for example, the fights that preoccupy Congress, those that consume weeks or months of congressional staff time, are typically contests between competing companies or industries.

While corporations are increasingly writing their own rules, they are also being entrusted with a kind of social responsibility or morality. Politicians praise companies for acting "responsibly" or condemn them for not doing so. Yet the purpose of capitalism is to get great deals for consumers and

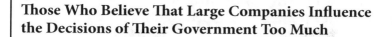

Those Who Believe That Large Companies Influence the Decisions of Their Government Too Much

Country	Percentage
Poland	57%
Japan	57%
Sweden	65%
Netherlands	69%
Italy	72%
Belgium	74%
Czech Republic	74%
Spain	74%
Russia	75%
Great Britain	75%
India	76%
Australia	78%
South Korea	79%
Turkey	79%
Mexico	79%
Germany	80%
Canada	80%
United States	82%
Brazil	84%
France	85%
Argentina	85%

TAKEN FROM: Ipsos Reid, "Not So Happy New Year Wishes: To National and Multinational Corporations from the World's Most Engaged, Influential," January 2, 2008.

investors. Corporate executives are not authorized by any-one—least of all by their investors—to balance profits against the public good. Nor do they have any expertise in making such moral calculations. Democracy is supposed to represent the public in drawing such lines. And the message that companies are moral beings with social responsibilities diverts public attention from the task of establishing such laws and rules in the first place.

It is much the same with what passes for corporate charity. Under today's intensely competitive form of global capitalism, companies donate money to good causes only to the extent the donation has public relations value, thereby boosting the bottom line. But shareholders do not invest in firms expecting the money to be used for charitable purposes. They invest to earn high returns. Shareholders who wish to be charitable would, presumably, make donations to charities of their own choosing in amounts they decide for themselves. The larger danger is that these conspicuous displays of corporate beneficence hoodwink the public into believing corporations have charitable impulses that can be relied on in a pinch.

The purpose of capitalism is to get great deals for consumers and investors.

The Purpose of Democracy

By pretending that the economic success corporations enjoy saddles them with particular social duties only serves to distract the public from democracy's responsibility to set the rules of the game and thereby protect the common good. The only way for the citizens in us to trump the consumers in us is through laws and rules that make our purchases and investments social choices as well as personal ones. A change in labor laws making it easier for employees to organize and negotiate better terms, for example, might increase the price of products and services. My inner consumer won't like that very much, but the citizen in me might think it a fair price to pay. A small transfer tax on sales of stock, to slow the movement of capital ever so slightly, might give communities a bit more time to adapt to changing circumstances. The return on my retirement fund might go down by a small fraction, but the citizen in me thinks it's worth the price. Extended unemployment insurance combined with wage insurance and job training could ease the pain for workers caught in the downdrafts of globalization.

Let us be clear: The purpose of democracy is to accomplish ends we cannot achieve as individuals. But democracy cannot fulfill this role when companies use politics to advance or maintain their competitive standing, or when they appear to take on social responsibilities that they have no real capacity or authority to fulfill. That leaves societies unable to address the trade-offs between economic growth and social problems such as job insecurity, widening inequality, and climate change. As a result, consumer and investor interests almost invariably trump common concerns.

The vast majority of us are global consumers and, at least indirectly, global investors. In these roles we should strive for the best deals possible. That is how we participate in the global market economy. But those private benefits usually have social costs. And for those of us living in democracies, it is imperative to remember that we are also citizens who have it in our power to reduce these social costs, making the true price of the goods and services we purchase as low as possible. We can accomplish this larger feat only if we take our roles as citizens seriously. The first step, which is often the hardest, is to get our thinking straight.

In the United States and the United Kingdom, Democracy Threatens Capitalism

Anatole Kaletsky

In the following viewpoint, Anatole Kaletsky argues that public response to the global financial crisis in the United States and the United Kingdom runs the risk of preventing the economic expansion necessary to end the crisis. Kaletsky maintains that a retreat from capitalism in response to the Great Depression led to disaster. He worries that the popular outrage against expansionary policies in democratic countries runs the risk of threatening a capitalist solution to the crisis. Kaletsky is an economist and editor-at-large of the Times, *a London newspaper.*

As you read, consider the following questions:

1. According to Kaletsky, President Barack Obama expressed outrage at what act by the insurance group, American International Group (AIG)?

2. Kaletsky claims that the public fury against bankers and the financial system raises what question?

3. What popular current beliefs about borrowing and spending, also popular in the 1930s, is the author worried about?

Anatole Kaletsky, "Are Democracy and Capitalism Incompatible? Public Hatred of Bankers and Their Booty Stands in the Way of the Expansion Needed to Stop World Economic Collapse," *The Times* (London, England), March 19, 2009, p. 26. Copyright © 2009 by *The Times* (London, England). All rights reserved. Reproduced by permission.

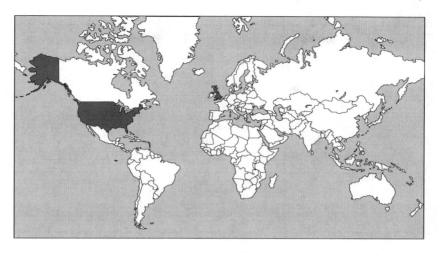

Three weeks ago in his address to Congress [February 24, 2009], President [Barack] Obama said: "In a time of crisis, we cannot afford to govern out of anger, or yield to the politics of the moment. I know how unpopular it is to be seen as helping banks when everyone is suffering from their bad decisions. But I also know that my job is to solve the problem."

The Hatred of Bankers

What has happened—not only in America but also in Britain—to this promise of a calm, pragmatic response to the world's economic problems? This week Mr Obama expressed outrage at the $165 million bonuses paid by AIG [American International Group], the stricken insurance group, to executives in its financial products division who are responsible for most of its tens of billions of dollars in losses.

In Britain the row over [then chief executive of the Royal Bank of Scotland] Sir Fred Goodwin's pension continues to grow. And in both countries, hatred of bankers is making it difficult for governments to take further action to stabilise the banks and support economic growth.

The behaviour of the bankers who first blew up the world financial system and then proceeded to loot it is genuinely outrageous and deserves political retribution. But that should take the form of recovering the booty by the normal processes of law.

Hatred of bankers is making it difficult for governments to take further action to stabilise banks and support economic growth.

In Britain, the best approach would probably be for the Treasury and Financial Services Authority to launch civil lawsuits against Sir Fred and other senior bankers alleging negligence, breach of fiduciary duty and violation of numerous investment regulations by publishing misleading information about the financial condition of their companies.

Whether the Government would succeed in proving negligence is almost beside the point. The cost of the lawsuits alone, even if no damages were awarded, would be more than enough to ruin most bankers. And even those rich enough to bear the financial costs of defending themselves would have their personal lives destroyed by being dragged through the courts.

This was the fate of the totally innocent directors of Equitable Life [life insurance company] and of many guiltless members of Lloyd's [of London, an insurance company]. Faced with the threat of such legal trauma, Sir Fred and the other "guilty men" of the banking community would have overwhelming incentives to reach out-of-court settlements—voluntarily giving up all their pensions and other gains in exchange for immunity from legal action.

The Backlash Against Capitalism

But such legal chess games do not satisfy lynch mobs—especially in America, where public fury is turning not only against individual bankers but against the system as a whole.

Even Democratic congressmen are now calling for the resignation of the Treasury secretary, Tim Geithner, who has been in office for less than two months and is the only economic official confirmed so far by the Senate—and therefore quite literally the one man able to protect the country from total economic collapse.

This bloodlust raises a truly alarming question: Can capitalism and democracy survive side by side? Four months after Mr Obama's election the policy paralysis in Washington [DC] continues—and the backlash against the financial policies required to avert disaster becomes more vicious by the day.

This bloodlust raises a truly alarming question: Can capitalism and democracy survive side by side?

The Blame for the Great Depression

This brings to mind a disconcerting historical reality airbrushed away in the simplified picture presented by textbook economics: the people who are now blamed for the Great Depression of the 1930s and Japan's lost decade—Andrew Mellon, the US Treasury secretary in the early 1930s, and Yasushi Mieno, the governor of the Bank of Japan from 1989 to 1994—were not stupid, ignorant or wicked.

They were considered at the time the leading economists and financiers of their generation and were widely admired for their honesty and ethical standards. And they enjoyed widespread public support for their puritanical views about the virtues of saving, the dangers of creating future booms and the necessity of punishing and "purging" imprudent and unethical boom-time behaviour.

The confusion of moralism and economics led to disaster, as even schoolchildren are now taught. But many people also understood this in the 1930s.

[British economist] John Maynard Keynes campaigned for budgetary flexibility and abandonment of the gold standard for at least a decade before publishing his *The General Theory [of Employment, Interest and Money]* in 1936. And he was a genius of rhetoric as well as of economics. He could argue far more eloquently for expansionary policies than any of his latter-day disciples, from Mervyn King [governor of the Bank of England] and Ben Bernanke [chairman of the US Federal Reserve] down to humble journalistic scribblers such as myself.

He could explain his ideas with equal brilliance in the abstractions of Treasury mandarins or the straightforward language of common people: "Housewives of England, for every shilling you save, you put a man out of work for a day." But Keynes's arguments were ignored by democratic governments the world over. [British Prime Minister] Gordon Brown describes a document in the Treasury archives in which Keynes's proposals for saving Britain from depression were dismissed by the Permanent Secretary with three scribbled words: "Inflation, Extravagance, Bankruptcy."

Most people in the 1930s agreed with the Treasury that Keynes was irresponsible and deluded. And that is what many believe today—that a debt crisis cannot be cured by borrowing; that saving is virtuous while spending is wasteful; that printing money creates inflation and that the best response to recession is to fire government bureaucrats.

The Hazard of Democracy

If these beliefs become conventional wisdom among voters, then coping with the economic crisis will become as difficult as it was in the 1930s—at least for democracies. And here we come to the real horror.

In the 1930s only one country put expansionary policies fully into practice. [Adolf] Hitler's Germany, guided by the explicitly Keynesian economic thinking of its Finance Minister, Hjalmar Schacht, rapidly restored full employment by building the autobahns, even before it turned to rearmament.

The US and Britain, by contrast, never applied expansionary policies even in [President Franklin D.] Roosevelt's New Deal. It took Hitler's war to create the consensus required for the bold fiscal policies that pulled the democratic countries out of depression.

Now consider this: Is it coincidence that China is [the] only leading economy where growth seems assured and there is no doubt about the solidity of the banking system? So is democracy incompatible with bold economic expansion?

Obviously, I hope this is not true—and I am encouraged that for 250 years everyone who has bet against American democracy and capitalism has lost. But what if President Obama proves unable to unify America around an effective policy to pull itself out of recession? I can think of only one answer: We had better start learning Chinese.

Capitalism Improves the Lives of Women More Than Democracy Does

Michael D. Stroup

In the following viewpoint, Michael D. Stroup argues that when it comes to improving the welfare of women, capitalism fares better than democracy. Comparing increases in economic freedom with increases in political rights among countries with high levels of both and low levels of both, Stroup contends that when a country increases economic freedom—becoming more capitalistic—women see greater gains in well-being than when a country becomes more democratic by increasing political rights. Stroup is a professor of economics at Nelson Rusche College of Business at Stephen F. Austin State University.

As you read, consider the following questions:

1. What two countries does Stroup identify as having relatively high levels of both economic freedoms and political rights?

2. According to the author, a one-point increase of the economic freedom index (EFI) in a country with high levels of both economic and political freedom raises women's literacy rate by what percent?

3. According to Stroup, a one-point increase of the economic freedom index (EFI) in a country with low levels of both economic and political freedom raises women's literacy rate by what percent?

Capitalism and democracy are both known to improve the well-being of women. But which is more important? The social welfare of both men and women can be measured by health, education and employment, and the well-being of women in particular by gender-specific indicators, such as control of fertility. Poor countries generally rank lower than developed countries on all these social metrics, but they can implement public policies to improve conditions. Two major strategies have been tried: 1) market-oriented economic reforms and 2) democratic political reforms. The evidence suggests that institutional reforms that move an economy closer to capitalism have a greater positive influence on the well-being of women than political reforms that increase women's participation in decision making.

Measuring Sticks and Outcomes

A capitalistic, or economically free, society is one in which institutions are characterized by personal choice, voluntary exchange, freedom to compete and protection of person and property. It requires such public policies as open markets, limited government, stable monetary growth, free trade and a strong rule of law. Several indices exist for measuring the economic freedom of a society. One of the most popular is the Fraser Institute's economic freedom index (EFI). It uses objective data to rate more than 120 countries, from 1975 to the present. Academic studies have shown that a country's economic freedom has positive effects on many measures of economic progress, including investment, growth and income.

Freedom House produces a political rights index (PRI), based on their Freedom in the World survey. The PRI aggregates several factors related to political rights on a single scale, including the right to organize political parties, the significance of the opposition vote, and the realistic possibility of the opposition increasing its support or gaining power through elections. Studies have found mixed support for positive effects of political freedom on measures of human welfare.

There are large discrepancies among countries in economic and political freedom scores as averaged over the last two decades. The United States and Switzerland have relatively high levels of both economic freedoms and political rights, while Algeria and Burundi have relatively low levels of both types. On the other hand, Singapore and Bahrain have relatively higher levels of economic freedoms while allowing relatively fewer political rights. Argentina and Russia, until recently, had granted relatively more political rights while allowing relatively limited economic freedom.

Focusing on Specific Outcomes for Women

In order to determine the effects of economic freedom and political rights on women in particular, both the EFI and PRI were evaluated with respect to four outcomes: life expectancy, literacy rates, secondary education enrollment and labor force participation. In addition, many development studies point to the ability to determine family size and control the incidence of pregnancy as important aspects of the quality of life for women. Thus, fertility and use of contraceptives were also measured.

Where applicable, the outcomes were analyzed twice, once for the benefits of each freedom to women in an absolute sense, and once for the benefits women receive relative to the benefits to men. (Contraception use and fertility were only measured absolutely and secondary school enrollment and labor force participation were only measured relative to men.) All of these results were calculated after controlling for cross-country differences in per capita income.

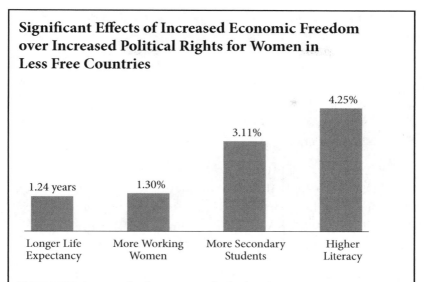

Significant Effects of Increased Economic Freedom over Increased Political Rights for Women in Less Free Countries

4.25% — Higher Literacy

3.11% — More Secondary Students

1.24 years — Longer Life Expectancy

1.30% — More Working Women

TAKEN FROM: Michael D. Stroup, "Which Is More Important for Women, Capitalism or Democracy?," National Center for Policy Analysis, *NCPA Brief Analysis*, no. 261, July 14, 2008.

In countries with comparatively high levels of both economic and political freedom:

- A one-point increase in a country's EFI score raises women's life expectancy by 1.2 years.

- A one-point increase in a country's EFI score raises women's literacy rate 3.9 percent.

- When compared to males, a one-point increase in a country's EFI score raises the proportion of female secondary school students by 2.4 percent, but has no significant effect on the labor force ratio.

Unlike the EFI scores, however, changes in PRI scores did not have a significant effect on any of the measures of well-being, with the exception of the female/male secondary school student ratio, where a one-point PRI increase raised the ratio 0.6 percent.

In countries with comparatively low levels of both economic and political freedom:

- A one-point increase in a less-free country's EFI score raises women's life expectancy by 1.2 years (the same as in economically and politically freer countries), but an increase in the PRI score has no statistically significant effect.

- A one-point increase in a less-free country's EFI score has a greater effect on the literacy rate among women than it does in freer countries, increasing women's literacy 4.25 percent; but again the PRI score is not significant.

- In comparison to males, a one-point increase in a less-free country's EFI score raises the proportion of female secondary school students by 3.1 percent and the proportion of females in the labor force 1.3 percent.

For these countries, the only significant effect of the PRI score was that a one-point increase in political rights reduced fertility rates by 0.03 children and increased contraceptive use by 0.50 percent.

Contrary to the claims of some development economists, capitalism yields more than just greater economic efficiency.

The Benefits of Economic Freedom

Economic freedom benefits women in additional ways. For example, multinational corporations competing for dependable, productive labor in developing countries implement nondiscrimination policies and training programs, on-site child care and other family-friendly policies that increase work opportunities for women.

Thus, contrary to the claims of some development economists, capitalism yields more than just greater economic efficiency. It also improves the well-being of women. The evidence implies that those societies that rely more heavily upon economic freedoms to promote women's well-being will be more successful than those societies that rely more heavily upon greater political rights to achieve social progress.

Conversely, if a country's government concentrates its efforts on increasing the efficacy of democratic policies in society, rather than on promoting greater economic freedom, it will likely produce smaller improvements in the quality of life for women. Additionally, it might be that governments pushing more political freedom—at the expense of economic freedom—are not quite as capable of generating public policies that effectively supply public goods and encourage social progress.

In Many Countries, Capitalism Exists Without Democracy

Paul Gottfried

In the following viewpoint, Paul Gottfried contends that it is not the case that all capitalist countries are democratic. Pointing to the examples of Singapore, China, and Russia, as well as historical Europe, he claims that a variety of political systems, including authoritarian ones, can exist along with capitalist economic systems. Gottfried also raises the concern that even in democratic capitalist states, democracy itself threatens the continuation of capitalism. Gottfried is Horace Raffensperger Professor of Humanities at Elizabethtown College in Pennsylvania and an adjunct scholar of the Ludwig von Mises Institute.

As you read, consider the following questions:

1. The author cites what country as one of the most successful examples of nondemocratic capitalism?

2. Gottfried contends that Germany's national debt is likely to increase fivefold in the next 20 years due to the cost of what?

3. What belief of the end-of-history theorists of the 1990s has not proven consistently true, according to the author?

History was supposed to have ended in 1989 with the triumph of Western-style democracy and capitalism. The fall of the Berlin Wall proved, at least to the satisfaction of many American pundits and academics, that economic and political liberty advanced hand in hand. Prosperity must bring freedom and vice versa, a virtuous cycle that would lead the developing world inexorably toward American ideals.

The Link Between Democracy and Capitalism

But after 20 years, an alternative scenario has arisen. "By shifting from Communist command economy to capitalism, China and Russia have switched to a far more efficient brand of authoritarianism," Azar Gat of Tel Aviv University argued in *Foreign Affairs*. These countries "could establish a powerful authoritarian-capitalist order that allies political elites, industrialists and the military; that is nationalist in orientation; and that participates in the global economy on its own terms." Indeed, our erstwhile Cold War [a period of tension between the United States and Russia during the second half of the 20th century] foes are doing well with their new economic systems. Russia under [Prime Minister Vladimir] Putin and China since the end of Maoism have both registered high rates of economic growth. In Russia, disposable income in the last six years has risen almost fourfold, while unemployment has gone down by more than half. There and in China, the vast majority express a high degree of satisfaction with the way the government has handled the economy.

This stands in sharp contrast to public opinion in America, where 82 percent of the population considers the country to be "headed in the wrong direction." As the events of recent weeks [September 2008] have shown, democratic capitalism—once imagined to be the unstoppable wave of the future for the entire world—now faces an uncertain tomorrow even in the West. Pat Buchanan [a conservative author and politician] noted in a recent column, "Liberal democracy is in a bear market. Is it a systemic crisis, as well?" If it is, might authoritarianism and capitalism soon seem to be natural complements, the way that free markets and democracy were once thought to be?

Advocates of "democracy plus free markets" typically favor some variation of capitalism that is fused with popular elections, religious and cultural pluralism, secularized political institutions, tolerance of homosexuality, and women's rights. These seem to be the necessary preconditions for economic and moral well-being and for a peaceful international community, since, according to this particular picture of human history, democracies never fight each other.

At least to some extent, the identification of democracy with prosperity is true. The Fraser Institute's *Economic Freedom of the World: 1975–1995* and other more recent surveys show the correlation between high standards of living and "democratic institutions." Even such heavily taxed and regulated "democratic" countries as Sweden and Norway boast some of the world's highest living standards, as well [as] extensive domestic and foreign investments in their economies. Welfare states such as Australia, Iceland, Canada, and Sweden also register respectable rates of economic growth. That is because these countries, like our own, are politically stable and still have relatively unfettered economies.

Democratic capitalism—once imagined to be the unstoppable wave of the future for the entire world—now faces an uncertain tomorrow even in the West.

Examples of Nondemocratic Capitalism

But there is no reason to think that only governments that are "democratic" in the current usage can provide political stability and good investment climates. Free markets are operating well in very different political systems. One of the most successful examples of nondemocratic capitalism is Singapore, which after winning independence in 1959 flourished under the firm hand of Lee Kuan Yew, who was prime minister or senior minister from 1959 until 2004. Lee has always stressed economic productivity and very low taxes. But in a 1994 interview with Fareed Zakaria, he pronounced his opposition to "Western democratic imperialism." While acknowledging that the U.S. has some "attractive features," such as "the free and open relations between people regardless of social status, ethnicity or religion" and "a certain openness in argument about what is good or bad for society," Lee expressed doubts about the American way "as a total system." "I find parts of it totally unacceptable," he told Zakaria, "guns, drugs, violent crime, vagrancy, unbecoming behavior in public—in sum the breakdown of civil society. The expansion of the right of the individual to behave or misbehave in public as he pleases has come at the expense of an orderly society."

In Lee's country—and in Asia more generally—they do things differently: "In the East the main object is to have a well-ordered society so that everyone can have a maximum enjoyment of his freedom. This freedom can only exist in an ordered state and not in a natural state of contention of anarchy." Lee had admired the U.S. in the past, but given the "erosion of the moral underpinnings" and the "diminution of personal responsibility" that has since taken place in recent decades, he has since changed his view of American democracy for the worse.

Contemporary Russia and China provide even more striking examples than diminutive Singapore of relatively free markets under authoritarian governments. But one need not look so far afield—the historical milieu in which capitalism arose in Europe supplies ample evidence closer to home. Industrial development in the West began long before European societies became "democratic" in the contemporary sense. Until the

20th century, women didn't vote, nor did they hold extensive property rights. In many of the countries in which industrialization and the rise of the bourgeoisie first occurred, there was nothing like separation of church and state. And most of the Western societies that were undergoing industrial development in the mid or late 19th century were not particularly tolerant toward labor unions: workers' strikes were often broken up by the police or the military. The Western societies that created free markets and expansive economies sometimes look almost medieval, as viewed from the perspective of contemporary "democracy." Yet these societies typically had freer—that is, less regulated—markets than our own modern states.

Free markets are operating well in very different political systems.

Democratic Capitalist States

Conversely, present-day notions of democratic equality and what the state must do to promote that value may eventually preclude the possibility of relatively free markets. Despite their costly welfare states, Western democracies have so far been able to survive as wealth-producing countries, and this situation might have prevailed forever—if certain conditions of late democracy had not come along. In particular, feminist attitudes toward childbearing and the modern democratic state's affinity for mass immigration have clouded the future of free markets. To regard these culturally revolutionary features as merely accidental accompaniments of democratization is naïve. They are inherent in the claims made by modern democracies to being pluralistic, egalitarian, and universalistic.

The current version of democracy benefits from consumer capitalism inasmuch as public administration needs the financial resources and consumer goods produced by the market to maintain social control. Consumer societies also serve the goal of democratic socialization—that is, the creation of "democratic," as opposed to "authoritarian," personalities—by encouraging a materialistic way of life. As Daniel Bell argues in *The Cultural Contradictions of Capitalism*, other things being equal, democratic-capitalist societies work against pre-modern institutions and values. A stress on consumption and on fashionable commodities leads to a condition of life characterized by the availability of ever-increasing goods and the association of social rank with their acquisition. Living in this manner nurtures both individual-centeredness and openness to change. These are values that democratic educators are happy to emphasize in order to weaken and replace traditional, pre-democratic communities.

But there are limits to how far democratic welfare states will go to sustain capitalism. Democracy's support of feminism, for example, creates short-term benefits but also long-term headaches for the economy. While today's working women earn and spend more than their predecessors who were not part of the labor force, they are also less focused than earlier generations on child-rearing, and are unable or unwilling to devote as much time and energy to their offspring. Among the results of women's emancipation from the family, particularly in Europe, has been a graying of the native population and the need to import a foreign, largely Third World, labor force. The rationale for this step has been to pay for retirement funds and social services, although more recently this policy has also been justified as helping to enrich the culture.

Contradictions of Democratic Capitalism

The gamble of importing unskilled immigrants to make up for the birth dearth has not paid off for Germany. Because of that country's bloated welfare state, its national debt is now 11 times higher than it was in 1972, and it is likely to increase fivefold in the next 20 years in order to provide social services

The Future of Liberal Democracy

Capitalism's ascendancy appears to be deeply entrenched, but the current predominance of democracy could be far less secure. Capitalism has expanded relentlessly since early modernity, its lower-priced goods and superior economic power eroding and transforming all other socioeconomic regimes. . . . In the post–Cold War era (just as in the nineteenth century and the 1950s and 1960s), it is widely believed that liberal democracy naturally emerged from these developments, a view famously espoused by Francis Fukuyama [an American political scientist]. Today, more than half of the world's states have elected governments, and close to half have sufficiently entrenched liberal rights to be considered fully free.

But the reasons for the triumph of democracy, especially over its nondemocratic capitalist rivals of the two world wars, Germany and Japan, were more contingent than is usually assumed. Authoritarian capitalist states, today exemplified by China and Russia, may represent a viable alternative path to modernity, which in turn suggests that there is nothing inevitable about liberal democracy's ultimate victory—or future dominance.

Azar Gat,
"The Return of Authoritarian Great Powers,"
Foreign Affairs, *July/August 2007.*

to the new immigrants, the vast majority of whom are either unemployed or earning-impaired. Unemployment is now many times what it was in the 1970s. And the demographic collapse is only worsening. A prominent economist and one-time adviser to the Christian Democrats, Meinhard Miegel, in his monograph *Die Deformierte Gesellschaft*, draws a gloomy picture of a society that is falling on the skids materially, in a way that Freedom House and the Fraser Institute have avoided noticing. By 2200, if present trends continue, Germany will have the population that it did in 1800, but the demographic distribution will be the opposite: in 1800, most Germans were below 40 years of age; already today 24 percent are 60 or older.

Democracy today, with its emphasis on equality and pluralism, is an agent of social disintegration.

Although there are special circumstances in the German case, such as the costs of national reunification, most of Germany's problems are characteristic of other Western societies. Women marrying late or choosing not to marry at all, low fecundity rates, and the welcoming of unskilled immigrants have all become endemic in the West. Democracy today, with its emphasis on equality and pluralism, is an agent of social disintegration.

It's also bad business. Although a modern democratic system can coexist with capitalism in the short and even middle terms, the two will eventually clash. Their contradictions are too glaring not to surface. Expanding social programs, the lopsided statistical distribution of young and old caused by the very democratic feminist movement, and the importing of unskilled labor are bound to increase popular demands for income redistribution. Our own country now stands at the threshold of new social spending such as government-controlled health care. While it might be hard to demonstrate that such developments have always inhered in a welfare-state democratic regime, one can easily comprehend how modern democracy reached its present state here and in Europe.

Capitalism Does Not Need Democracy

Can authoritarian governments conceivably do better than modern democracies as frameworks for capitalist economies? Certainly the old idea that capitalist development inevitably leads to political freedom has fewer adherents today than it did at the end of the Cold War. Robert Kagan, in his new book *The Return of History and the End of Dreams*, no longer treats the movement toward liberal democracy as "the unfolding of ineluctable processes," though he still calls for the U.S. to form a "league of democracies"—an arrangement that his admiring blurber, [senator and 2008 presidential candidate] John McCain, intends to put himself in charge of—to force the world to be free.

Once the reader looks beyond Kagan's search for enemies against whom the "democracies" can mobilize their laggard populations, however, one sees that he makes several relevant points. Authoritarian powers like Russia and China can effectively integrate free market economies into their nationalist projects. Economic freedom does not necessarily require the adoption of liberal or democratic institutions. The belief that had driven the end-of-history theorists of the 1990s, that movement toward the free market would be accompanied by political liberalization, has not proven consistently true, and the exceptions might be more important than the embodiments of the rule.

Autocratic capitalism may prove a transitory phenomenon.

Although Kagan ignores the changing meaning of his god-terms "liberal" and "democratic," he correctly perceives the degree to which politics can control economics, even in a recognizable market economy. Not all capitalist economies will lead to the election of Barack Obama or [former prime minister of the United Kingdom] Tony Blair. Indeed, in some societies a thriving economy may go hand in glove with a favored Russian Orthodox Church, the veneration of the last tsar and his family, or evocations of the glory of the Ming dynasty. To his credit, Kagan admits that capitalism does not always lead in the political direction he wants it to go. Market economies can be a valuable asset to any kind of government. Even those that prefer to rule by the stick have come to recognize the need for carrots.

A Possible Transitory Phenomenon

Even so, autocratic capitalism may prove a transitory phenomenon, for the simple reason that authoritarian regimes are not likely to endure. Israeli political scientist Amos Perlmutter, the author of *Modern Authoritarianism*, argues that despotic governments rule in societies that are only imperfectly modernized: They have typically depended for their establishment on (often shifting) alliances made with the peasantry, military, established churches, and elements of the working class. Over time, such regimes either give way to other, similar orders— often as the result of military coups—or else they evolve, like [dictator Francisco] Franco's Spain, Syngman Rhee's South Korea in the 1950s, and [Augusto] Pinochet's Chile in the 1980s, into middle-class constitutional states. Perlmutter does not have an ax to grind against authoritarian regimes, which often provide the breathing space for economic and political change. But he views them as stepping stones to periodic instability or else to democratic capitalism. Within this view, one does not have to agonize over a Singaporean exception, since Lee's attempt to blend economic growth with Confucian culture may not have any significance outside of his region. Lee may have produced an exotic flower that does not flourish in other climates.

It goes without saying that should authoritarian-capitalist states metamorphose into new democratic-capitalist regimes, they will soon be subject to all of the problems familiar to the West. And these difficulties will set in far faster than they did in our country because American cultural values will soon be swamping these fledgling democracies—by example, if not by force. Given their longtime totalitarian pasts—and in China's case, far-flung, dense population—the modern malaise may take root in authoritarian lands more slowly than in more Westernized countries such as Japan. But the Chinese and Russian cases are not yet illustrations of a stable, long-term "authoritarian capitalism." Most likely, Putin and the Chinese Communists will eventually give way to "democratic capitalist" governments or to periodic regime changes followed, in the best of circumstances, by further economic growth. Without nurturing any illusions about the supposed friendship between democracy and capitalism, there is no compelling reason to treat autocratic capitalism as a permanent arrangement. The friendliest climate for economic freedom may have existed in pre-democratic Western societies in the 19th century. But that too proved to be a transition to something else, a new "democracy" with whose consequences we are still contending.

In China, Capitalism Exists Without Political Democracy

Boris Johnson

In the following viewpoint, Boris Johnson argues that it is false that the Chinese are moving toward democracy. Johnson claims that even the young Chinese are in favor of authoritarianism and are reluctant to embrace change. Nonetheless, Johnson contends, the Chinese have embraced capitalism, and China is experiencing huge economic growth. He concludes that because China lacks both soft and hard power (partly due to a failure to embrace democracy), there is little risk of China becoming the next world power. Johnson is a columnist and has served as mayor of London since 2008.

As you read, consider the following questions:

1. The author claims that after a visit to China he changed his mind about what?

2. Johnson contends that the Chinese have a 4,000-year-old respect for what?

3. The Chinese per capita gross domestic product (GDP) is what amount per year, according to Johnson?

It was towards the end of my trip to China that the tall, beautiful Communist Party girl turned and asked the killer question. 'So, Mr Boris Johnson,' she said, 'have you changed

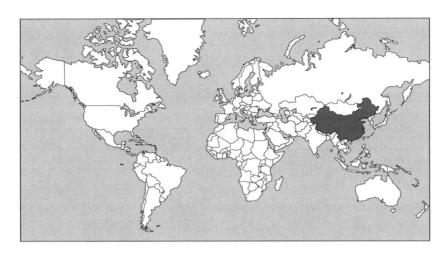

your mind about anything?' And I was forced to reply that, yes, I had. Darned right I had.

I had completely changed my mind about the chances of democracy in China. Before flying to Beijing I had naively presumed that the place was not just exhibiting hysterical economic growth, but was about to enter a ferment of political change. I had assumed that [former British prime minister] Tony Blair was right when, in 2005, he went there and announced that the 1.3 billion Chinese were on an 'unstoppable march' towards multiparty politics. I now know that he was talking twaddle, and, what is more, that his Foreign Office advisers knew it.

Before flying to Beijing I had naively presumed that the place was not just exhibiting hysterical economic growth, but was about to enter a ferment of political change.

Like most reporters of my generation I spent a certain amount of the 1980s in the former Soviet Union and Eastern Europe, and we all remember that sense of suppressed mutiny, how easy it was to find people willing to prophesy over late-night vodka or slivovitz that one day the lid would blow off the cooker and Western-style democracy would be ushered in. Well, it's not that way in China today.

Political Views of the Chinese

I came away with an impression of a gloriously venal capitalist explosion being controlled by an unrepentant Bolshevik system, and—this is the key thing—with the patriotic support of almost all the intelligentsia. One night I had dinner with a charming group of young Chinese professionals, all of whom had studied in England, and who you might therefore expect to have drunk deep of our liberal political potion. I began by pointing out that I was that exotic British phenomenon, a 'shadow' minister. Of course, I said patronisingly, you don't have an opposition, do you? 'No,' they smiled. 'Well,' I said, 'wouldn't it be a good thing?' I waved my arms at the panorama of Shanghai behind us, where illuminated pleasure boats chugged along the river, and the fangs of 300 skyscrapers probed the night, soon to be joined by 300 more.

'What if you get fed up with the people running this show? Wouldn't you like to kick them out? Kick the bastards out, eh?' I stabbed my chopsticks at a passing squid.

'Actually, no,' said Oswald, a nice guy with specs who had studied at Keble [College]. He didn't think the British system would work in China at all. 'I think a one-party state is good for China right now,' he said, and the squid, more elusive in death than in life, shot from my fumbling sticks and lay on the tablecloth in a metaphor of Western incomprehension.

'But what about Chairman [of the Communist Party of China] Mao [Zedong]?' I asked. I had been stunned, in Beijing, to find his warty visage still looming over the entrance to the Forbidden City, and to see the crowds of reverential citizens still visiting the mausoleum of a man who, in his 27-year reign, was responsible for the deaths of 70 million people and who therefore, in the evil tyrant stakes, knocks [German leader Adolf] Hitler and [Soviet Communist leader Joseph] Stalin

145

into a cocked hat. Surely it was time to break with the legacy of Mao? This time it was a spiky-haired young lawyer called Harry who dealt gently with my misconceptions.

'Different times produce different heroes,' he said. 'We cannot put ourselves in the position that Mao was in.' 'But what if you want to get involved in politics,' I asked. 'What do you do?' 'You must join the Communist Party, and work for the government,' said Lucy, a girl on my left. 'It is a great honour to join the Communist Party. You must be a very bright student.'

Before you accuse me of talking to the wrong people, let me assure you that I found the same story everywhere: not so much a defence of Chinese communism, or totalitarianism, but a patient refusal to accept my glib assumptions of the superiority of Western pluralism; because the more I harped on, the more resolute my interlocutors became in their defence not so much of the system but of China itself.

The Role of Journalists in China

In Shanghai we went to an enormous and lavishly equipped college of journalism, and after we had all swapped business cards (which must be exchanged sacramentally, with both hands and a small kung-fu bow) there was a slide show of all the distinguished foreigners who had been there, ranging from [US president] Ronald Reagan to [British politician] Margaret Hodge, and then it was my cue to make a small speech of thanks. I explained again that I was an opposition politician, and that I believed it was important to keep up my journalism as a way of getting my message across. This dual role I chose to describe by what I thought was a happy Mao-style aphorism. 'You could say that I combine the functions of dog and lamp-post!'

As I spoke I could hear the British Council man on my left groan and whisper 'no, no', and around the table, on the faces of the tutors of Chinese journalism, there was frank mystification. Later on that evening, when I was trying to explain it to the Communist Party girl, it was some time before she grasped what in Western liberal democracies constitutes the proper relationship between the journalist (dog) and the politician (lamp-post), and if you want to understand why my sally [witty remark] fell so thunkingly flat, there is a very simple reason.

It is a cliché worth repeating that the Chinese have a colossal, 4,000-year-old respect for authority.

In today's China the dogs are still so respectful of the lamp-posts that the editor of one big paper recently admitted that he gave bonuses to reporters whose work was praised by the Ministry of Information. In many cities the journalists turn up at press conferences and are given little cash-stuffed envelopes to thank them for being there. When I asked the lecturers in journalism to name their professional heroes, they looked utterly bemused, eventually naming Edgar Snow, the American stooge and hagiographer of Mao. At the end of our session at the journalism college a pale, intense academic came up privately and said of course I was right to say that journalism should root out corruption, 'but we must also care about stability,' he said, and there is the nub.

It is a cliché worth repeating that the Chinese have a colossal, 4,000-year-old respect for authority, and a deep unwillingness to be seen to do anything that is extrovert, embarrassing, satirical, flatulent, foolish, irreverent—in fact, they have been wholly bypassed by the European Enlightenment. They have a different concept of the relation between the individual and society, and a distrust of any kind of seditious argument, let alone satire. It's not so much that they would be shocked by [French writer] Voltaire. They would be shocked by [Athenian playwright] Aristophanes. With every group of students I

Wealth in China

The form which capitalism takes can vary in different parts of the world. In China, the state still has a more important role to play than in the West. Although the ruling party is the only permitted political organisation, how much longer this continues to be the case remains to be seen.

According to *Forbes* magazine (8 October 2007), in 2007 China, with 108, ranked second behind the US in the number of dollar billionaires. Yang Huiyan ($16.02 billion) came [to the] top of the Chinese list, while Xu Rongmao ($7.03 billion) came second.

Vincent Otter, "A Socialist Visits Capitalist China,"
Socialist Standard *(UK), September 2010.*

---

tried, in a flat-footed way, to raise issues of academic and intellectual freedom, in particular the notorious restrictions on the Internet.

Wasn't it absurd that the state was blocking access to Wikipedia, the online encyclopaedia, particularly since it seemed to have been written by Maoists anyway? And every time the students responded that it wasn't such a problem, that there were ways round it, I was struck by their apathy, their acquiescence, their un-Tiananmen [un-revolutionary] spirit, their willingness to accept the arguments for 'stability' and the public good: to the point where I suddenly felt it was pointless and boorish of me to keep levelling these implicit criticisms of my hosts.

Capitalism Without Democracy

The Chinese are gluttons for gilts and bonds and calls and puts and leveraged buyouts; but they aren't very keen on the idea of elections, and instead of nipples on their billboards they would much rather have the luscious Technicolor full-frontal advertising for machine tools that greets the passenger arriving at Shanghai station. They want to do it the authoritarian way, the Chinese way, partly because the fear of disorder is so strong, and partly, frankly, because the rest of the world does not yet provide an overwhelming advertisement for democracy.

If the Chinese want to prove to themselves that elections lead to chaos and kleptocracy, they need only look at Russia. If they want to reassure themselves that Blair and the neocons are wrong, and that democracy is not one of those sow-anywhere plants, they only have to look at the disaster of Iraq. In fact, the more people like me insist on rabbiting on about democracy, the more the Chinese must inwardly resolve to vindicate their own specialness and their own solution, complete with prison camps, mass capital punishment, and getting fired if you have more than one baby; not least since the present Chinese formula seems to be such a roaring success.

The Chinese are gluttons for gilts and bonds and calls and puts and leveraged buyouts; but they aren't very keen on the idea of elections.

They have averaged growth of 9 per cent over the last 25 years; they are creating the fastest bullet train in the world as well as 30 nuclear reactors, and hundreds of millions of peasants are still moving to the cities to stand in plimsolls and suits on girders hundreds of feet up in the cause of the most enormous boom in construction and industrialisation the world has ever seen. Even in my own area of special interest, higher education, the Chinese story is astonishing: There are now 1,800 state universities (there are about 90 in the UK) as well as 1,300 technical colleges, and the Chinese don't have any of the British addiction to state funding.

This may be technically a Communist country, but in some universities 50 per cent of total funds are fees paid by the students, their families and even their neighbours (whereas top-up fees will contribute about 2 per cent of Cambridge's budget). Oh, and just to freeze your marrow further, the Chinese turn out millions of highly qualified scientists and mathematicians, at a time when 30 per cent of British university physics departments have closed in the last eight years. You cannot hope to pass the gaokao, the fearsome Chinese university entrance exam which is sat by eight million 18-year-olds a year (and failed by three million of them), unless you have the equivalent of a B or better at math A level.

China's Lack of Soft and Hard Power

The longer you spend in the new China, watching the oxy-acetylene lamps on the building sites at 3 a.m., the clearer it is that [American economist] Francis Fukuyama was wrong when, in 1989, he pronounced that the fall of Soviet communism meant the end of history. Systematically, methodically, and with the connivance of their entire political establishment and their growing bourgeoisie, the Chinese are making a mockery of the claim that free-market capitalism and democracy must go hand in hand. Which is why, finally, I do not altogether go along with those who have suggested that the next century will belong to China, or that China will somehow rule the planet.

It is true that the new China is a wonderful place, and certainly a lot better than the old Communist China, and with the growing international renown of their economic performance the Chinese are gaining in confidence and spiritual hope. It is also true that Chinese competition is a huge challenge for us in Western Europe, and certainly a useful hobgoblin for those of us who think that Gordon Brown's Labour Party is eroding our competitive edge.

But with Chinese per capita GDP [gross domestic product] still only $1,000 per year, and with all the corruption and inefficiency still generated by a one-party state, I am not yet convinced that we need to force all our children to learn Mandarin. If China is really to rule the world, she will need two things that America now has in superabundance: hard power and soft power.

The Chinese are making a mockery of the claim that free-market capitalism and democracy must go hand in hand.

As a military power, China is still relatively insignificant (her defence spending is smaller than that of the UK); and as for soft power—cultural projection abroad—what can China boast, apart from the occasional arrival in London of the state ballet or the Beijing People's Circus? It is a tragic fact that every year thousands of Chinese undergo surgery to make their features more Western. To see how remote is the day of Chinese cultural dominance, ask yourselves how many Westerners would have surgery to make themselves look more Chinese.

Soft power—cultural influence—is ultimately impossible without an appealing international brand, and for the foreseeable future China's international brand will be vitiated by her domestic political arrangements. China will never rule the world as long as the Forbidden City is adorned with the face of the biggest mass murderer in history. In the words of [Beatles singer/songwriter] John Lennon, 'If you go carrying pictures of Chairman Mao/You ain't gonna make it with anyone anyhow.'

In Latin America, Democratic Countries Are Rejecting Capitalism

Naomi Klein

In the following viewpoint, Naomi Klein argues that although there have been attempts to forcibly bring neoliberal capitalism to Latin America through the use of shock doctrine, democratic movements are rejecting capitalism. Klein claims that democracies in Latin America have repeatedly rejected capitalism and chosen socialism, despite attempts from both inside and outside to defeat it, and political movements are becoming resistant to attempts to undermine democratic socialism. Klein is a journalist, syndicated columnist, and author of The Shock Doctrine: The Rise of Disaster Capitalism.

As you read, consider the following questions:

1. Klein claims that during the 1980s and 1990s, dictatorships in Latin America gave way to what?

2. The politicians that have been winning elections in Latin America recently are staunch opponents of what, according to the author?

3. Klein contends that in 2006 there were how many cooperatives in Venezuela, formed by recovering bankrupt businesses?

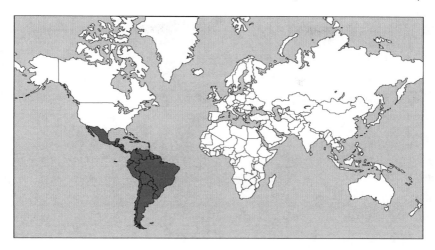

In one of his most influential essays, the late economist Milton Friedman articulated contemporary capitalism's core tactical nostrum, what I call the shock doctrine. He observed that "only a crisis—actual or perceived—produces real change. When that crisis occurs, the actions that are taken depend on the ideas that are lying around."

The Shock Doctrine

Latin America has always been the prime laboratory for this doctrine. Friedman first learned how to exploit a large-scale crisis in the mid-1970s, when he advised Chilean dictator Gen. Augusto Pinochet. Not only were Chileans in a state of shock following Pinochet's violent overthrow of Socialist President Salvador Allende; the country was also reeling from severe hyperinflation. Friedman advised Pinochet to impose a rapid-fire transformation of the economy—tax cuts, free trade, privatized services, cuts to social spending and deregulation. It was the most extreme capitalist makeover ever attempted, and it became known as a Chicago School revolution, since so many of Pinochet's top aides and ministers had studied under Friedman at the University of Chicago. A similar process was under way in Uruguay and Brazil, also with the help of University of Chicago graduates and professors, and a few years later, in Argentina. These economic shock therapy programs were facilitated by far less metaphorical shocks—performed in the region's many torture cells, often by US-trained soldiers and police, and directed against those activists who were deemed most likely to stand in the way of the economic revolution.

In the 1980s and '90s, as dictatorships gave way to fragile democracies, Latin America did not escape the shock doctrine. Instead, new shocks prepared the ground for another round of shock therapy—the "debt shock" of the early '80s, followed by a wave of hyperinflation as well as sudden drops in the prices of commodities on which economies depended.

In Latin America today, however, new crises are being repelled and old shocks are wearing off—a combination of trends that is making the continent not only more resilient in the face of change but also a model for a future far more resistant to the shock doctrine.

When Milton Friedman died last year [2006], the global quest for unfettered capitalism he helped launch in Chile three decades earlier found itself in disarray. The obituaries heaped praise on him, but many were imbued with a sense of fear that Friedman's death marked the end of an era. In Canada's *National Post*, Terence Corcoran, one of Friedman's most devoted disciples, wondered whether the global movement the economist had inspired could carry on. "As the last great lion of free market economics, Friedman leaves a void. . . . There is no one alive today of equal stature. Will the principles Friedman fought for and articulated survive over the long term without a new generation of solid, charismatic and able intellectual leadership? Hard to say."

It certainly seemed unlikely. Friedman's intellectual heirs in the United States—the think-tank neocons [neoconservatives] who used the crisis of September 11 [2001] to launch a booming economy in privatized warfare and "homeland security"—were at the lowest point in their history. The movement's political pinnacle had been the Republicans' takeover of the US Congress in 1994; just nine days before Friedman's death, they lost it again to a Democratic majority. The three key issues that contributed to the Republican defeat in the 2006 midterm elections were political corruption, the mismanagement of the Iraq War and the perception, best articulated by Jim Webb, a winning Democratic candidate for the US Senate, that the country had drifted "toward a class-based system, the likes of which we have not seen since the nineteenth century."

The Attempt to Defeat Democratic Socialism

Nowhere, however, was the economic project in deeper crisis than where it had started: Latin America. Washington [DC] has always regarded democratic socialism as a greater challenge than totalitarian communism, which was easy to vilify and made for a handy enemy. In the 1960s and '70s, the favored tactic for dealing with the inconvenient popularity of economic nationalism and democratic socialism was to try to equate them with Stalinism [policies associated with Soviet premier Joseph Stalin], deliberately blurring the clear differences between the worldviews. A stark example of this strategy comes from the early days of the Chicago crusade, deep inside the declassified Chile documents. Despite the CIA [Central Intelligence Agency]-funded propaganda campaign painting Allende as a Soviet-style dictator, Washington's real concerns about the Allende victory were relayed by [then US National Security Advisor] Henry Kissinger in a 1970 memo to [President Richard] Nixon: "The example of a successful elected Marxist government in Chile would surely have an impact on—and even precedent value for—other parts of the world, especially in Italy; the imitative spread of similar phenomena elsewhere would in turn significantly affect the world balance and our own position in it." In other words, Allende needed to be taken out before his democratic third way spread.

But the dream Allende represented was never defeated. It was temporarily silenced, pushed under the surface by fear. Which is why, as Latin America now emerges from its decades of shock, the old ideas are bubbling back up—along with the "imitative spread" Kissinger so feared.

By 2001 the shift had become impossible to ignore. In the mid-'70s, Argentina's legendary investigative journalist Rodolfo Walsh had regarded the ascendancy of Chicago School economics under junta rule as a setback, not a lasting defeat, for the Left. The terror tactics used by the military had put his country into a state of shock, but Walsh knew that shock, by its very nature, is a temporary state. Before he was gunned down by Argentine security agents on the streets of Buenos Aires in 1977, Walsh estimated that it would take twenty to thirty years until the effects of the terror receded and Argentines regained their footing, courage and confidence, ready once again to fight for economic and social equality. It was in 2001, twenty-four years later, that Argentina erupted in protest against IMF [International Monetary Fund]-prescribed austerity measures and then proceeded to force out five presidents in only three weeks.

Washington has always regarded democratic socialism as a greater challenge than totalitarian communism.

"The dictatorship just ended!" people declared at the time. They meant that it had taken seventeen years of democracy for the legacy of terror to fade—just as Walsh had predicted.

In the years since, that renewed courage has spread to other former shock labs in the region. And as people shed the collective fear that was first instilled with tanks and cattle prods, with sudden flights of capital and brutal cutbacks, many are demanding more democracy and more control over markets. These demands represent the greatest threat to Friedman's legacy because they challenge his central claim: that capitalism and freedom are part of the same indivisible project.

Democratic Opposition to Capitalism

The staunchest opponents of neoliberal economics in Latin America have been winning election after election. Venezuelan president Hugo Chávez, running on a platform of "Twenty-First-Century Socialism," was re-elected in 2006 for a third term with 63 percent of the vote. Despite attempts by the [George W.] Bush administration to paint Venezuela as a pseudo-democracy, a poll that year found 57 percent of Venezuelans happy with the state of their democracy, an approval rating on the continent second only to Uruguay's, where the left-wing coalition party Frente Amplio had been elected to government and where a series of referendums had blocked major privatizations. In other words, in the two Latin American states where voting had resulted in real challenges to the Washington Consensus, citizens had renewed their faith in the power of democracy to improve their lives.

Ever since the Argentine collapse in 2001, opposition to privatization has become the defining issue of the continent, able to make governments and break them; by late 2006, it was practically creating a domino effect. Luiz Inácio Lula da Silva was re-elected as president of Brazil largely because he turned the vote into a referendum on privatization. His opponent, from the party responsible for Brazil's major sell-offs in the '90s, resorted to dressing up like a socialist NASCAR driver, wearing a jacket and baseball hat covered in logos from the public companies that had not yet been sold. Voters weren't persuaded, and Lula got 61 percent of the vote. Shortly afterward in Nicaragua, Daniel Ortega, former head of the Sandinistas, made the country's frequent blackouts the center of his winning campaign; the sale of the national electricity company to the Spanish firm Unión Fenosa after Hurricane Mitch, he asserted, was the source of the problem. "Who brought Unión Fenosa to this country?" he bellowed. "The government of the rich did, those who are in the service of barbarian capitalism."

In November 2006, Ecuador's presidential elections turned into a similar ideological battleground. Rafael Correa, a 43-year-old left-wing economist, won the vote against Álvaro Noboa, a banana tycoon and one of the richest men in the country. With Twisted Sister's "We're Not Gonna Take It" as his official campaign song, Correa called for the country "to overcome all the fallacies of neoliberalism." When he won, the new president of Ecuador declared himself "no fan of Milton Friedman." By then, Bolivian President Evo Morales was already approaching the end of his first year in office. After sending in the army to take back the gas fields from "plunder" by multinationals, he moved on to nationalize parts of the mining sector. That year in Chile, under the leadership of President Michelle Bachelet—who had been a prisoner under Pinochet—high school students staged a wave of militant protests against the two-tiered educational system introduced by the Chicago Boys. The country's copper miners soon followed with strikes of their own.

The staunchest opponents of neoliberal economics in Latin America have been winning election after election.

Political Movements in Latin America

In December 2006, a month after Friedman's death, Latin America's leaders gathered for a historic summit in Bolivia, held in the city of Cochabamba, where a popular uprising against water privatization had forced Bechtel [Corporation] out of the country several years earlier. Morales began the proceedings with a vow to close "the open veins of Latin America." It was a reference to Eduardo Galeano's book *Open*

Veins of Latin America: Five Centuries of the Pillage of a Continent, a lyrical accounting of the violent plunder that had turned a rich continent into a poor one. The book was published in 1971, two years before Allende was overthrown for daring to try to close those open veins by nationalizing his country's copper mines. That event ushered in a new era of furious pillage, during which the structures built by the continent's developmentalist movements were sacked, stripped and sold off.

Today Latin Americans are picking up the project that was so brutally interrupted all those years ago. Many of the policies cropping up are familiar: nationalization of key sectors of the economy, land reform, major investments in education, literacy and health care. These are not revolutionary ideas, but in their unapologetic vision of a government that helps reach for equality, they are certainly a rebuke to Friedman's 1975 assertion in a letter to Pinochet that "the major error, in my opinion, was . . . to believe that it is possible to do good with other people's money."

Though clearly drawing on a long rebellious history, Latin America's contemporary movements are not direct replicas of their predecessors. Of all the differences, the most striking is an acute awareness of the need for protection from the shocks that worked in the past—the coups, the foreign shock therapists, the US-trained torturers, as well as the debt shocks and currency collapses. Latin America's mass movements, which have powered the wave of election victories for left-wing candidates, are learning how to build shock absorbers into their organizing models. They are, for example, less centralized than in the '60s, making it harder to demobilize whole movements by eliminating a few leaders. Despite the overwhelming cult of personality surrounding Chávez, and his controversial moves to centralize power at the state level, the progressive networks in Venezuela are at the same time highly decentralized, with power dispersed at the grassroots and community levels, through thousands of neighborhood councils and co-ops. In Bolivia, the indigenous people's movements that put Morales in office function similarly and have made it clear that Morales does not have their unconditional support: the barrios will back him as long as he stays true to his democratic mandate, and not a moment longer. This kind of network approach is what allowed Chávez to survive the 2002 coup attempt: when their revolution was threatened, his supporters poured down from the shantytowns surrounding Caracas to demand his reinstatement, a kind of popular mobilization that did not happen during the coups of the '70s.

It stands to reason that the revolt against neoliberalism would be in its most advanced stage in Latin America.

Latin America's new leaders are also taking bold measures to block any future US-backed coups that could attempt to undermine their democratic victories. Chávez has let it be known that if an extremist right-wing element in Bolivia's Santa Cruz province makes good on its threats against Morales's government, Venezuelan troops will help defend Bolivia's democracy. Meanwhile, the governments of Venezuela, Costa Rica, Argentina, Uruguay and Bolivia have all announced that they will no longer send students to the School of the Americas (now called the Western Hemisphere Institute for Security Cooperation)—the infamous police and military training center in Fort Benning, Georgia, where so many of the continent's notorious killers learned the latest in "counterterrorism" techniques, then promptly directed them against farmers in El Salvador and autoworkers in Argentina. Ecuador, in addition to closing the US military base, also looks set to cut its ties with the school. It's hard to overstate the importance of these developments. If the US military loses its bases and training programs, its power to inflict shocks on the continent will be greatly eroded.

The Revolt Against Neoliberalism

The new leaders in Latin America are also becoming better prepared for the kinds of shocks produced by volatile markets. One of the most destabilizing forces of recent decades has been the speed with which capital can pick up and move, or how a sudden drop in commodity prices can devastate an entire agricultural sector. But in much of Latin America these shocks have already happened, leaving behind ghostly industrial suburbs and huge stretches of fallow farmland. The task of the region's new left, therefore, has become a matter of taking the detritus of globalization and putting it back to work. In Brazil, the phenomenon is best seen in the million and a half farmers of the Landless [Workers'] Movement (MST), who have formed hundreds of cooperatives to reclaim unused land. In Argentina, it is clearest in the movement of "recovered companies," 200 bankrupt businesses that have been resuscitated by their workers, who have turned them into democratically run cooperatives. For the cooperatives, there is no fear of facing an economic shock of investors leaving, because the investors have already left.

Chávez has made the cooperatives in Venezuela a top political priority, giving them first refusal on government contracts and offering them economic incentives to trade with one another. By 2006 there were roughly 100,000 cooperatives in the country, employing more than 700,000 workers. Many are pieces of state infrastructure—toll booths, highway maintenance, health clinics—handed over to the communities to run. It's a reverse of the logic of government outsourcing: rather than auctioning off pieces of the state to large corporations and losing democratic control, the people who use the resources are given the power to manage them, creating, at least in theory, both jobs and more responsive public services. Chávez's many critics have derided these initiatives as handouts and unfair subsidies, of course. Yet in an era when [oil corporation] Halliburton treats the US government as its personal ATM for six years, withdraws upward of $20 billion in Iraq contracts alone, refuses to hire local workers either on the Gulf Coast or in Iraq, then expresses its gratitude to US taxpayers by moving its corporate headquarters to Dubai [in the United Arab Emirates] (with all the attendant tax and legal benefits), Chávez's direct subsidies to regular people look significantly less radical. . . .

It stands to reason that the revolt against neoliberalism would be in its most advanced stage in Latin America. As inhabitants of the first shock lab, Latin Americans have had the most time to recover their bearings, to understand how shock politics work. This understanding is crucial for new politics adapted to our shocking times. Any strategy based on exploiting the window of opportunity opened by a traumatic shock—the central tenet of the shock doctrine—relies heavily on the element of surprise. A state of shock is, by definition, a moment when there is a gap between fast-moving events and the information that exists to explain them. Yet as soon as we have a new narrative that offers a perspective on the shocking events, we become reoriented and the world begins to make sense again.

Once the mechanics of the shock doctrine are deeply and collectively understood, whole communities become harder to take by surprise, more difficult to confuse—shock-resistant.

Periodical and Internet Sources Bibliography

The following articles have been selected to supplement the diverse views presented in this chapter.

David Brooks	"The Larger Struggle," *New York Times*, June 15, 2010.
Tulin Daloglu	"Democracy, Capitalism: Disentangle the Ideals," *Washington Times*, October 21, 2008.
Financial Times	"Where Capitalism Trumps Democracy," October 1, 2007.
Robert W. Fogel	"Capitalism and Democracy in 2040," *Daedalus*, Summer 2007.
Bill George	"The U.S.'s Hidden Asset: Global Capitalism," *Bloomberg Businessweek*, August 5, 2007.
Stefan Halper	"The World of Market Authoritarianism," *American Spectator*, October 2009.
Michael A. Lebowitz	"Venezuela: A Good Example of the Bad Left of Latin America," *Monthly Review*, July/August 2007.
Vincent Otter	"A Socialist Visits Capitalist China," *Socialist Standard* (United Kingdom), September 2010.
Carl J. Schramm	"Can Democracy Survive Capitalism?" *Claremont Review of Books*, Fall 2009.
David D. Sussman	"Venezuela's Fork in the Road: Socialism or Capitalism?," *Christian Science Monitor*, November 21, 2008. www.csmonitor.com.
Gary Younge	"The People Have Spoken. Don't Let the Markets Shout Them Down," *Guardian* (United Kingdom), May 10, 2010.

GLOBALVIEWPOINTS

CHAPTER 4

Capitalism and Social Welfare Spending

Europe Should Not Abandon Its Social Model of Capitalism

Jeremy Rifkin

In the following viewpoint, Jeremy Rifkin argues that Europe should not abandon its capitalist model that balances the free market with social programs. Rifkin contends that, despite misperceptions, Europe is actually strong economically, especially when one considers that not all positive aspects are measured by gross domestic product. Rifkin warns against the adoption of the American model by the Europeans, concluding that to do so would result in problems. Rifkin is founder and president of the Foundation on Economic Trends and author of The European Dream: How Europe's Vision of the Future Is Quietly Eclipsing the American Dream.

As you read, consider the following questions:

1. What two countries does Rifkin claim have market economies with few controls and large disparities in income?

2. The author contends that Americans are richer than Europeans if you measure wealth in terms of what?

3. According to the author, what is the family savings rate in America?

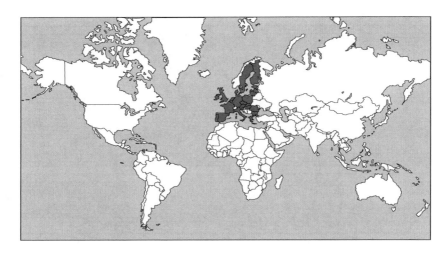

It would be unfortunate if the debate in the European Union [EU] became polarized around the issue of choosing between the American market model and the continental European social model. If that happens, you're just going to get more alienation and greater polarization. Both capitalism and socialism have strengths and weaknesses, and if you can take the strengths from each and use them, then each one is an antidote or counterbalance to the other within the same system. So it's not a question of whether you want capitalism or a socialist welfare state.

Socialism and Capitalism

Let's start with socialism. Its strength is solidarity—there is a collective responsibility for making sure that everyone is taken care of and that nobody is left behind. However, what socialist societies do not do well is to encourage individual initiative. Especially if you look at the Marxist version from the Bolshevik Revolution of 1917 up to the fall of the Berlin Wall. Individual initiative was brutally squelched and the entrepreneurial spirit and economic growth was dismal. Socialism doesn't stimulate self-interest, the entrepreneurial spirit or growth.

Capitalism, meanwhile, incontrovertibly stimulates self-interest, innovation, entrepreneurial growth and fosters development. That's its strongest point and it's something nobody would deny. Where capitalism stumbles, however, is in fairly distributing the fruits. It's complete fiction that the "invisible hand" will distribute the fruits. The fact is that if you let the market economy go unfettered without any controls, it will run wild and result in a "winner take all" society—and that's what you have in the US and, increasingly, the United Kingdom [UK].

To be fair, the Brits haven't totally followed the unfettered market model and I think Prime Minister Tony Blair is right that it's not right to accuse him of having done so. On the other hand, Britain has gone a long way towards undermining its social model. But the US and the UK also have the dubious distinction of moving more quickly towards greater disparity in income between rich and poor than any other OECD [Organisation for Economic Co-operation and Development] countries. They also have the fastest-growing crime rates. Britain is not anywhere near where we [the United States] are on the unfettered market. But if Britain or Europe let the markets go unfettered, they will end up with the American model.

The key is this: You need to continually stimulate the market because it's the engine of growth. At the same time, we need strong trade unions, strong political parties and a strong civil society that can act as an antidote in order to ensure the fruits are fairly distributed.

With capitalism, the logic in the boardroom is to cut your costs, and labor is a key one, so you're always trying to beggar the laborer in order to maximize shareholder value. But there's a contradiction built into a system. That is, when you're constantly trying to lower labor costs, you undermine income distribution and weaken consumption. If you're not distributing enough income, who's going to buy the goods and services being produced? You really need a strong counterbalance. On the flip side, there's a deadly creeping paternalism in the welfare state model that often results in people becoming more and more dependent on the state and losing their personal initiative.

Misperceptions About Europe

But I think there are a lot of misperceptions out there about the strengths of America versus Europe. If you measure the economy by GDP [gross domestic product], you could say, the US is doing well. But remember, the EU's GDP exceeded ours in 2003. So if the European Union is moribund and falling apart, if it's a museum filled with pampered workers, an aging population and inflexible labor, then how come its GDP exceeded our 50 states in 2003? Yes, they have a bigger population, but they also have a sizable GDP.

Here's the truth: The European Union is the largest exporter in the world—it's ahead of the United States and China. That will shock a lot of people. Europe's largest exporter, Germany, sells more goods abroad than either the US or China, and that's only one EU country. Europe is the largest internal market in the world; 61 of the world's largest 140 companies are based there. It dominates in banking and insurance, aerospace with Airbus, engineering, construction, and the chemical and food sectors. America leads in some pretty big industries, too—pharmaceuticals, automobile manufacturing, software and telecoms—but to say we're this big economic giant and Europe's falling apart? I'm sorry!

There's a lot more to an economy than GDP—and even there, Europe isn't so far behind the US.

Let me talk about how you measure a good economy. If you measure it by the paycheck, then we're 28 percent richer per capita than Europeans. But if you measure wealth by quality of life, then the EU 15 passed up America at least 10 years

The European Middle Class

Europe's workfare system has been grossly mischaracterized by Americans in thrall to a fundamentalist free market ideology. U.S. politicians are known for invoking the importance of "family values" and a "work hard, get ahead" creed. Indeed, the United States is known as the inventor of the middle class, the attractive ideal that a good life is within reach for the vast majority of people. But if America invented the middle class, Europeans have taken that good idea and run with it one giant step further. They have figured out how to set the middle class on a more solid and secure footing and put some meat on the bones of their family values. They also have fewer poor people; indeed, "old Europe" shows more economic mobility and more poor people joining the middle class than does the American "land of opportunity," completely turning convention on its head. Europeans have constructed their system so as to support families better and to minimize the personal risk for individuals in an age of globalized capitalism that has brought increasing economic insecurity.

Steven Hill, Europe's Promise:
Why the European Way Is the Best Hope in an Insecure Age.
Berkeley: University of California Press, 2010.

ago in some areas. America has the best graduate schools in the world—though there are some good ones in Europe—but on the elementary and secondary level, students in 18 European countries performed better than American students in mathematics. We're the only industrialized country other than South Africa that doesn't offer its citizens universal health care—we've got 45 million people uninsured. We have fewer doctors per capita. The EU 15 population lives a year longer than we do and they have a much lower infant mortality because they have less poverty. Europe does have serious poverty and you do see it, but it's not as bad as in the US, where one out of four kids lives below the poverty line. When it comes to leisure time, we get an average of 5 to 10 days off a year while Europeans get four to six weeks off as a right mandated by law. Americans often say the Europeans are not as productive, but the OECD figures show that from the late 50s to mid 90s, the EU 15 countries had higher growth in productivity per hour almost every year. We did catch up in the late 1990s and we dramatically passed up Europe over the past three years [2002–2005]. But now Europe is going to be introducing the same IT [information technology] revolution we did in the next three to five years and will likely catch back up and may even go ahead of America again in productivity growth per hour.

Even in 2003, seven EU countries, including France and Germany, had higher productivity per hour than the US. They just choose to work fewer hours and make less money. If you look at safe communities, we have four times the homicide rate and 2 percent of the male working population is currently in prison. So there's a lot more to an economy than GDP—and even there, Europe isn't so far behind the US.

The Call to Abandon the European Model

The big problem in Europe right now is that a chorus of people—especially the neoconservatives and euroskeptics—are saying that even if there is a European Dream with a global vision and humane social programs, we have to wake up. The economy stinks, unemployment is high, euroskleurosis has set in and while we don't want to give up the dream, we can't really afford to continue with it. We've got to go to the American model. It's unfettered, it's market driven, it's brutal, it's draconian, it's Darwinian, but the Americans know how to grow an economy and create jobs.

But there is no positive correlation between eliminating all your social programs and a positive economy—there's only a negative correlation. If you eliminate the social benefits, you get negative GDP—more crime, more prisons, deteriorating health care, deteriorating infrastructure and greater pollution. A lot of the European countries and their social programs are too paternalistic and they need to be streamlined the way the Scandinavians have done it. Indeed, the economic successes of the Scandinavians have shown that you don't have to eliminate your social net in order to grow your economy—you can also find growth by streamlining the net.

There needs to be a balance between personal accountability and social solidarity. You can't be so dependent on the state that you no longer have any initiative. And you can't be so abandoned by society that you're all on your own and there's no helping each other.

Problems with the American Model

If you look at the American economy in a detached way, there's no doubt that the unfettered market produces some innovation and growth. But the truth is that the recent economic growth seen in the US has been, in large part, the result of a massive increase in consumer debt. The US came out of the 1989–92 recession by issuing credit cards. We went on a huge credit binge and we basically kept the American economy and the whole global economy afloat on consumer credit and American consumers continuing to buy.

The cost of this was the depletion of the family savings rates of millions of Americans—we had an 8 percent family savings rate in 1990 and it's nearly at zero today [2005]. We have millions of Americans who currently spend more than they make each year. More Americans this year will file for bankruptcy than for divorce, or get a heart attack, or get diagnosed with cancer, or graduate college. It's out of control. After we maxed out our credit cards, we refinanced our home mortgages, which was made easy by the low interest rates of the past five years. Now the interest rates have gone up and even the *Economist* recently worried that the US real estate bubble, the biggest in history, could burst [which it did in 2008].

And when Americans depleted their personal savings, President [George W.] Bush gave us a tax cut to give us more discretionary income. He had to make this money available because wages have been stagnant for 25 years and the broken unions no longer have the clout to negotiate a fair wage package with employers. The result of Bush's tax cut is that we now have record government deficits.

We have millions of Americans who currently spend more than they make each year.

All these problems are manifested in our currency. What I always ask my neoconservative friends is this: If Europe is so moribund and America so economically strong, why is the dollar continuing to devalue against the euro? It's because the investment community says we don't think the economic fundamentals are sound enough to guarantee pay off.

I keep telling my European friends that this is what you'll get if you go with the American model. You'll get a winner-takes-it-all system, a greater disparity in income, you'll have increased poverty. You'll get debt for your family. The only other country that has really followed our lead is Britain, and it now has the worst consumer debt ratio in the world—an achievement it has accomplished in just five years. The average Brit spends 120 percent of his or her income.

In the United States, Social Insurance Balances the Harms of Capitalism

Mark Thoma

In the following viewpoint, Mark Thoma argues that in a capitalist system, social insurance programs implemented by the government play the role of softening the blows of economic busts. Thoma claims that programs such as unemployment compensation, Social Security, and Medicare actually increase economic efficiency. Furthermore, he claims that the benefits of the programs outweigh the costs to society and, thus, argues against cutting these programs. Thoma is professor of economics at the University of Oregon and a columnist for The Fiscal Times.

As you read, consider the following questions:

1. Thoma contends that although capitalism delivers a high average rate of growth, it is vulnerable to what?
2. The author claims that what common misconception exists about social insurance programs?
3. According to Thoma, what other kind of argument reinforces the economic argument for helping the unfortunate?

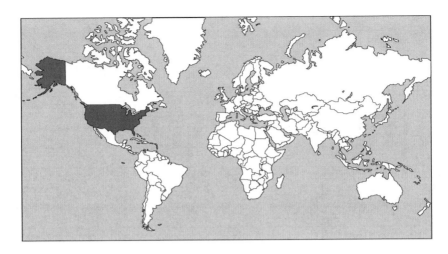

The recent [January 2011] appointment of Bruce Reed, the executive director of President [Barack] Obama's National Commission on Fiscal Responsibility and Reform, as Vice President [Joe] Biden's chief of staff is the latest signal that the administration plans to endorse many of the Commission's recommendations. Since one target for deficit reduction appears to be Social Security and social insurance programs more generally, it's essential to understand the important role that social insurance plays in the economy.

The Role of Social Insurance

There is no economic system yet discovered that can outperform capitalism when it comes to producing a vibrant, growing, dynamic, and innovative economy. Capitalism provides the goods and services that people want, for the most part, at the lowest possible cost.

However, while capitalism delivers a high average rate of output growth, it is also vulnerable to business cycles, and the busts that inevitably follow the booms can be quite costly. People who diligently show up for work every day can suddenly and unexpectedly lose their jobs as poor economic conditions cause businesses to fail. In addition, technology, globalization, or changes in tastes can leave people jobless and without the means to support their families even though they did nothing to deserve such a fate. Social insurance is a way to ease the costs for the unlucky workers who are hurt by the tides of capitalism.

In a capitalist system, as people compete with others to try and get ahead, they are motivated in ways that yield benefits for themselves and for the larger society. This is part of the edge that capitalism has over other systems. However, some people are unable to compete on an acceptable footing due to illness or old age. Social insurance can help here as well.

Social insurance is a way to ease the costs for the unlucky workers who are hurt by the tides of capitalism.

When someone loses a job through no fault of their own, we provide relief through unemployment compensation. If someone is born with a condition that limits their ability to compete in a market system, society is willing to help. Similarly, when old age takes its toll and people can no longer compete effectively for jobs, jobs that are needed to pay medical and other bills, we do not turn our backs, instead we give help in the form of Social Security and Medicare.

Government Intervention Increases Efficiency

Some people worry that social insurance programs such as unemployment compensation, Social Security, and Medicare take away the incentive to get ahead, the incentive that helps to make capitalism tick. Won't those being taxed to pay for the programs work less, and won't those receiving, say, unemployment compensation be less motivated to find work?

It is a common misconception that these programs necessarily reduce economic efficiency. In fact, to the extent that social insurance provides a service that people are willing to

Views on Significant Cuts to Federal Programs as of February 2011

Is significantly cutting the funding to this program totally unacceptable, mostly unacceptable, mostly acceptable, totally acceptable, or you're not sure?

	Totally unacceptable	Mostly unacceptable	Mostly acceptable	Totally acceptable	Not Sure
Medicaid, federal health care for the poor	35	32	23	9	1
Medicare, federal health care for seniors	46	30	16	7	1
Social Security	52	25	16	6	1
Unemployment Insurance	20	35	30	13	2

TAKEN FROM: Peter Hart and Bill McInturff, "Study #11091," NBC News/*Wall Street Journal* Survey, February 2011, p. 15.

pay for but cannot get due to market failures, social insurance improves economic efficiency.

Insurance markets are plagued by market failures such as adverse selection and moral hazard, and when these problems are severe enough the private sector will provide much too little of the insurance. In such cases, there is a role for government to play in resolving the problem. Efficiency is defined, in part, as the economy providing the goods and services that people want and are willing to pay for. Hence, when the government intervenes and makes up for the failure of private markets to provide these goods and services in sufficient quantity, it doesn't reduce efficiency, it increases it.

If anything, we need more social insurance, not less.

The Benefits of Social Insurance

We cannot fully insulate people from every inequity or run of bad luck, and it is possible for governments to provide more than the optimal amount of insurance against life's ups and downs. But even if social insurance programs are not executed perfectly by government, the important question is whether the benefits exceed the costs. One only has to look at our history—what happened to the elderly, the sick, and the unemployed before we had such insurance—to see its great value. We were much worse off, on net, before social insurance existed, and we would certainly be worse off without it today.

When Congress begins looking for ways to balance the budget, social insurance programs will be an easy target. But, if anything, we need more social insurance, not less. Globalization and technological change are making the world more uncertain, our experience with the Great Recession highlights the risk of busts in a capitalist system, and the problems associated with health and aging will always be present.

In addition, as we become wealthier as a society, we should be able to provide more help when illness strikes, when age slows us down, or when workers are cast aside as the economic system adjusts over time. And the moral argument for helping the unfortunate, especially in an era of ever increasing inequality, reinforces the economic reasons to help. As pressures to cut the budget continue to mount, we should not forget the important role that social insurance plays in easing the burdens that fate and time cast our way.

The United States Should Reduce Government Involvement in Social Welfare

Jim Manzi

In the following viewpoint, Jim Manzi argues that the social welfare system in America needs to be reformed. Manzi claims that although it is not reasonable to suppose that the welfare system can be eliminated, government involvement can be simplified and reduced. Manzi suggests reducing the role of the government and increasing the role of the market in education, Social Security, health care, and other welfare programs, suggesting some specific reforms where the government plays the role of regulator rather than provider. Manzi is a senior fellow at the Manhattan Institute and chairman of an applied artificial intelligence software company.

As you read, consider the following questions:

1. Manzi claims that the majority of the primary public budget for federal, state, and local governments in the United States is spent on what four items?
2. Which two components of the rationale for the welfare state does the author claim are legitimate government functions?

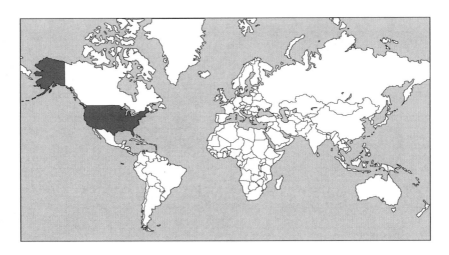

3. What is the key reason the United States has not implemented a scheme to provide money to individuals to maintain their own individual safety net, according to Manzi?

The West has built an edifice of markets and free political institutions through a combination of luck, work, foresight, and painful trial-and-error learning, and this has produced once-unimaginable prosperity. But that achievement faces a constant undertow of resistance. It is essential for those who defend market institutions not to mistake this resistance for a defective temperament or malign intent on the part of those who display it, but rather to realize that it is, in part, an inevitable manifestation of human nature. This tension sits at the root of the debate about the line between government authority and individual initiative, and a contemporary capitalist democracy must find a way to manage it.

The Welfare System

Governments in advanced democracies have deployed several overlapping strategies to ease the anxieties of capitalism. Among the most important are appeals to patriotism and other noneconomic bases of social cohesion, explicit support for nonmarket institutions such as traditional families, and investments in the development of human capital. All are useful, but this combination of strategies never works perfectly or completely. Hence the creation of the welfare system, a complex of government-funded programs including pensions, health care subsidies, transfer payments, and unemployment insurance. Public schools are dual-purpose institutions; they build human capital but also perform many social welfare functions.

The welfare system represents the majority of government spending in most modern, advanced nations. Even in the United States, with its ideological commitment to capitalism, spending on pensions, health care, education, and welfare accounts for a majority of the primary public budget across the total of federal, state, and local governments.

The welfare system represents the majority of government spending in most modern, advanced nations.

The problems of the welfare system are well understood by conservatives. First, there is the moral hazard created by providing for needs such as retirement savings that individuals could otherwise meet on their own. Another is provider capture, in which the public servants become important political players in their own right, as witness teachers' unions that use the public school system for their own narrow, self-interested ends. Still another problem is the habituation of the people to protection from uncertainty by a benevolent external power, a condition that can result in broad corrosion of initiative and the partial conversion of an entrepreneurial culture into a managerial one.

In sum, the welfare state can undermine the very capitalist system it is intended to support.

Elimination of the Welfare State

There is an obvious conflict between the methods for managing the tension between markets and human nature that conservatives prefer (appeals to patriotism and reliance on private institutions, such as families) and those that contemporary liberals prefer (welfare programs). Should conservatives simply advocate unwinding the whole apparatus of the welfare state in favor of exclusive reliance on private institutions and patriotism? Should we not only repeal Obamacare [referring to President Barack Obama's health care strategy], but also eliminate Medicare and Medicaid? Instead of privatizing Social Security, should we get rid of it?

The welfare state appears to be concomitant with the growth that capitalism creates.

It is possible, of course, that the development of the modern welfare state has been the result of a terrible wrong turn. Had it not reached full flower in Europe as various Marxian and other collectivist ideologies were being promulgated, or had the United States somehow avoided the "contamination" of the New Deal, perhaps the welfare state as we know it would never have come into being. Alternatively, one might argue that the welfare system was useful or necessary in years gone by, but that today's higher level of absolute wealth, technological achievement, and social evolution has made it obsolete. But it would be foolhardy, from a conservative perspective, to eliminate a system so central to day-to-day life and long-term planning—and especially to do so all at once, acting on an unproved theory.

While it is always possible that some future society will find a way to cultivate widespread wealth and stability without a welfare system, or that existing welfare systems will wither away, the welfare state appears to be concomitant with the growth that capitalism creates. As far as can be determined from history, the idea of an advanced capitalist society without a welfare system is misplaced nostalgia—or more accurately, an anachronism. It is like wishing for a commercial jet aircraft without wing stabilizers.

Goals for Reforming Welfare

If it is not advisable to eliminate the welfare system, we can at least understand reforms to it as attempts to create a check on a check. We want a welfare system as one part of a political economy that manages the conflict between capitalism and human nature in a fashion that achieves our shared goals, while putting a minimum of drag on market productivity and growth.

We should develop a set of goals to guide our efforts at reforming the welfare system. First, the primary purpose of the system should be to support capitalism, not to oppose it. Second, we should seek the system's maximum alignment with the elements of human nature that make us want it in the first place. Together, these two criteria simply mean that we should be as informed as possible about the costs and benefits created by the welfare system as we seek the greatest possible benefit for each unit of theoretically forgone growth that we invest in it. Third, we should attempt to shoot ahead of the duck by modifying the welfare system in a fashion that anticipates foreseeable changes in society and technology while leaving us maximum flexibility to respond to unforeseeable changes. This flexibility should include the possibility of dissolving our current welfare system or transforming it into programs that would be unrecognizable to us today.

Changes in America

America is a very different place than it was in the first half of the 20th century, and this has led to severe dislocations between the original design of our welfare programs and today's needs. For one thing, we are vastly wealthier. The simple lack of available food and shelter that in America persisted into the Great Depression is extremely rare today for any physically and mentally competent person who is willing to abide by the most basic social norms. Individual conduct is the primary driver of contemporary deprivation. Further, the ratio of old to young is crucially different. The money to pay for retirement spending (including late-life health care) must either come from one's own accumulated savings or be taken from somebody else. When the latter approach takes a tiny bite from many younger people's paychecks, it is not a critical political problem, but if the cost becomes an appreciable share of income as the ratio of workers to nonworkers rises, it becomes politically unsustainable.

We are fast approaching that point in the United States today. What are often called "promises" to workers are in fact merely current entitlement rules changeable at any time by any future Congress, and they cannot go unaltered without massive tax increases. As the private sector has already realized, we are moving from a "defined benefit" to a "defined contribution" world.

Another important development is greater diversity in the population, across many dimensions. There is far less agreement on how people should live their lives today than there was among the politically relevant population 50 years ago. In practical terms, this has meant the dissolution of the traditional family model for large swathes of American society.

A final relevant change is that Americans, especially the middle class, are far better educated than they were decades ago, and are used to having and managing many more choices enabled by information and technology.

The Rationale for the Welfare State

What hasn't changed is the basic rationale for the welfare state: It is a way of managing the tension between human nature and capitalism. All of the major elements of the welfare system—pensions, health care, education, and welfare payments—share a common architecture that combines them. Unbundling these five components—and understanding each one separately—can open up the path to achieving the goals of the welfare state in a modern environment.

First, welfare programs provide a safety net: a fail-safe provision of important goods that represents some roughly agreed-upon minimum baseline of subsistence for any member of the society. Second, they incorporate some element of risk pooling (and, more generally, economies of scale) beyond what is implied by the safety net: spreading out the costs of falling victim to some horrible disease in old age, for example. Third, these programs also may require prudent behavior on the part of beneficiaries. For example, Social Security requires that wage earners forgo some consumption today in order to provide funds for retirement. Fourth, the programs may redistribute wealth beyond what is required by the first two goals. Fifth and finally, they may be a mechanism for the government to provide certain goods directly, as in the case of traditional public schools.

Even if it made sense to bundle these functions in 1935, does it today?

What hasn't changed is the basic rationale for the welfare state: It is a way of managing the tension between human nature and capitalism.

A Safety Net and Risk Pools

The first two components—provision of a safety net and the exploitation of economies of scale, such as risk pools—are legitimate government functions. But bundling them has an enormous drawback: It hides the transfer of wealth from the prudent to the imprudent. This is especially problematic in the modern environment. The safety net and risk pools should be different programs.

For example, Social Security provides a safety net for old people who have been extremely unlucky, unwise, or unproductive. It is also a mechanism to force almost all workers to save for retirement—prudently consuming less today—and pool their savings. These two components were bundled to build a political coalition for the program, but the bundling obscures the income redistribution from richer workers to poorer ones that is embedded in Social Security's benefit schedules, which provide higher returns on the first dollars of worker earnings and lower returns on the last dollars. This, in turn, exacerbates the moral hazard of the program.

Instead, we should have a defined-contribution pension program requiring individuals to contribute a reasonable proportion of their income (though some flexibility should be allowed) to an array of investment vehicles to which they hold property rights. In addition, the government should offer a safety net specifically for those who end up destitute in old age. Unlike a safety net for people of working age, it should not have a work requirement. It should also not attempt to guarantee for all the income of those who have prudently saved for retirement but instead be a true minimum safety net. This is welfare for old people, and should not be conflated with a pension scheme.

Whether the government should engage in the fourth component—pure redistribution of wealth for reasons of equity or justice—is a thorny philosophical question. In practice, the contemporary American electorate has a very limited appetite for it. But to the extent that such redistribution is desired, it should be done explicitly and outside the other programs of the welfare system.

The Form for Government Benefits

Finally, when it comes to the fifth component—operation of a government bureaucracy to deliver goods—it is often useful to separate the *specification* of welfare benefits from their *provi-*

sion. For several decades, a goal of the libertarian Right has been to voucherize social programs so that the government provides the cash but allows private firms to compete in markets to provide the services. But this is not always as practical as it sounds.

School vouchers, for example, are premised on the idea that a marketplace for K–12 schools will both increase productivity (i.e., allow us either to increase the measured performance of schools at any given level of expenditure, or to achieve a given level of performance at lower cost) and provide a greater diversity of options to better meet different students' needs. One can imagine a wide array of specialized schools—with an arts or a mathematics focus, for example. Further extension of this idea would upend the model of school as a building that students in homogeneous age groups go to each day. By the voucherizing logic, students (or at least families) know their own needs and can better meet them than the state can with its one-size-fits-all approach—a reason to allow trial-and-error learning, which will improve the overall system with time.

The moral legitimization of the welfare system requires that the recipients earn their benefits and use them in a way that comports with the idea of the good life held by the taxpayers.

This sounds fantastic, and it is, in both senses of that term. It leads to the obvious question of why we should limit school spending to whatever some government entity decides to call "education." If individuals are the best judges of their welfare, why not let them decide how to spend this money? Taking the logic to its conclusion, we should ask: Why bother even to have such categories as school subsidies, health care subsidies, and all the rest? Instead, why don't we estimate the costs of a safety-net income, plus the costs of buying catastrophic insurance, and provide that amount of money to everyone in our society?

This idea has arisen again and again, on both the right and the left, beginning in the 1960s. Examples of such proposals include Milton Friedman's negative income tax (1962), Robert Theobald's guaranteed income (1966), James Tobin's guaranteed income (1965), R. J. Lampman's subsidy plan (1967), Edward Schwartz's guaranteed income, the negative income tax proposed by President [Lyndon B.] Johnson's Income Maintenance Commission (1969), President [Richard] Nixon's Family Assistance Plan (1969), George McGovern's $1,000-a-year plan (1972), and HEW's [Department of Health, Education, and Welfare's] Income Supplementation Plan (1974). The idea constantly resurfaces even today in academic discussions, and is being pursued seriously by the current coalition government in the United Kingdom. The key reason we haven't implemented such a scheme in the United States is that we are afraid that many recipients would not work and then would blow the money on Cheetos, beer, and big-screen TVs. In more academic language, the moral legitimization of the welfare system requires that the recipients earn their benefits and use them in a way that comports with the idea of the good life held by the taxpayers who provide the funds.

Public Schools with Partial Privatization

Though this logic is most relevant for safety-net functions, which tend statistically to have the most irresponsible recipients, it also applies to the provision of welfare benefits to the middle class under the rationale of risk-pooling and economies of scale. To return to the example of K–12 schools, the focus on true privatization has been both doctrinaire and artificial. If school choice ever grows beyond Tinkertoy demonstration projects, taxpayers will appropriately demand that a range of controls be imposed on the schools they are funding.

Would we allow families to use vouchers to send children to schools that taught no reading or mathematics, but only bomb-making, or that offered lavish "support payments" to parents that were, in effect, bribes? No, we would inevitably—and justifiably—have a fairly detailed set of regulations, along with inspection, adjudication, and enforcement mechanisms. At that point, what would be the difference between such "private" schools and "public" schools that were allowed greater flexibility in hiring, curriculum, and student acceptance, and had to compete for students in order to capture funding? Little beyond the label.

Publicly funded private schools is an oxymoron, but greater flexibility to meet different needs and to improve general performance through market competition can nonetheless be found in a public school system involving parental choice and the freedom of schools to operate outside of collective bargaining agreements and other restrictions. The most basic institutional requirements of a market would be present: consumer choice and widely distributed buying power on the demand side, capacity and flexibility on the supply side.

With such reforms under way, the next role for the government would be to provide information and truth in labeling, a classic market support. Suppose the federal government established a comprehensive national exam by grade level to be administered by all schools and universities that receive any federal money, and required each school to publish all results, along with detailed data about its budget, performance, and so forth, each year. Secondary, profit-driven information providers, analogous to equity analysts, would arise to inform decision making. The federal role in education would be very much like that of the SEC [US Securities and Exchange Commission] in securities markets: to ensure that each school published accurate, timely, and detailed data.

The next logical extension would be to let schools make profits and thereby pay returns to investors. One reason the market scaled up Starbucks from a mere idea to thousands of stores within about one decade, while promising education innovations proceed glacially, is that a fire hose of capital could be aimed at Starbucks once it demonstrated its profitability. While ongoing, massive public expenditures on education can partially serve this purpose now and in the future, the free flow of investment would replace the existing capital stock of school buildings and equipment faster than would normal political processes. Such schools would become something like publicly regulated utility companies that can issue debt and equity instruments to raise capital while still having to meet defined regulatory objectives.

For each of the programs we would face the same need to create market institutions that produce the benefits of freedom, competition, and trial-and-error learning.

Building Market Institutions

We would, in the end, get something like a partially privatized school system, but we would have to go through the hard work of building market institutions rather than just waving a magic wand of vouchers at the problem. The trick is to be able to execute a sequence of steps each of which must both make progress toward the goal and demonstrate practical improvement in and of itself. The sequence I propose is: 1) allow parents to choose among public schools, with funding following students, and reform the chartering process so that it is far easier to establish new schools without collective bargaining agreements; 2) institute consistent national annual testing for all schools that receive government funding, and publish the results along with other performance information; and 3) allow schools to operate at a profit in order to create incentives for private investment. More precisely, this is the vision that would animate the first steps of the journey. We could modify our plan of action as we proceeded and learned what worked and what did not.

The same basic argument applies to each major welfare program. Conservatives often argue that we should privatize Social Security. But we would surely regulate what investment vehicles would be allowed—otherwise, I could "invest" in a retirement portfolio of Cheetos, beer, and big-screen TVs. As with government-funded schools, we would need a set of regulations and a means of enforcing them. If we wanted to replace Medicare with health-savings accounts, we would face a similar problem.

Obviously, there will be challenges unique to each of these programs. For example, the degree of existing government entanglement varies widely. In the United States, the lack of an enormous government-operated physical-delivery infrastructure for health care and pensions (outside of specialized areas like the VA [Department of Veterans Affairs] hospital system) means that such a transition should be logistically simpler with health care than it would be with education. But for each of the programs we would face the same need to create market institutions that produce the benefits of freedom, competition, and trial-and-error learning, while to some degree regulating conduct in a way that is consistent with our vision of the good life.

Japan's Model of Ethical Capitalism Promotes Advanced Welfare

Japan Economic Foundation

In the following viewpoint, the Japan Economic Foundation (JEF) argues that Japan's unique model of capitalism stems from its idealistic traditions. JEF claims that whereas many capitalist models only emphasize individualism in their market models, Japan promotes welfare economics, balancing the gains of capitalism with advanced welfare policies. JEF suggests that Japan's model of capitalism with caring could provide a positive model of capitalism for the world. JEF was established to deepen mutual understanding between Japan and other countries through activities aimed at promoting economic and technological exchanges.

As you read, consider the following questions:

1. The Japan Economic Foundation claims that Japan was the world's second largest economic power during what period?
2. The Japan model of capitalism is close to the model of capitalism put forth by whom?

Japan Economic Foundation, "Rethinking Capitalism in Era of Global Recession," *Japan Spotlight: Economy, Culture, and History*, vol. 29, no. 6, November/December 2010, pp. 34–39. Copyright © 2010 Japan Economic Foundation. All rights reserved. Reproduced by permission.

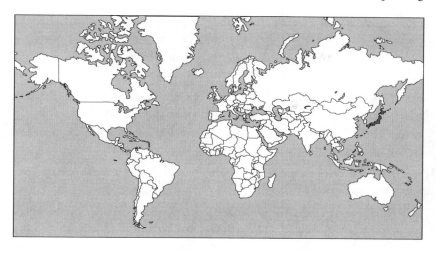

3. The author claims that Japan should respond to the trend toward having fewer children by taking what three actions?

Since the economic crisis, negative opinions have been appearing throughout the world, including distrust of the "market economy" and the "modern economics" behind it, and even of GNP [gross national product] and economic growth itself. Meanwhile, noneconomic values such as "culture" and "ethics" appear to be being overvalued as well. We feel uneasy about such extreme trends. In contrast to the rapacious capitalism symbolized by the subprime loan frenzy that sparked off the financial crisis, traditional capitalism since the time of Adam Smith [a Scottish political economist] emphasizes ethics, based on assumed economic activity.

The Market Economy

We should not forget that the "market economy" that assumes minimum ethics has brought many benefits to humanity. Through the activation of the market economy, humankind has learned that economic prosperity makes it hard to wage wars. Through economic globalization, many developing countries have achieved economic development, and poverty is gradually disappearing from the world to some extent. In the post-WW2 [World War II] development of the Japanese economy, the activation of both market competition and innovation has played a large role. Equal income distribution was also brought about in many cases by the market mechanism. In fact, often the inequality of different incomes for the same ability was the result of nonmarket factors such as regulation and employment practices.

We feel it is important to have a balanced opinion in regard to the market economy, a fundamental element of capitalism. Also, it is inappropriate to make light of economic growth as a materialistic concept or, in an extreme position, to regard the "economy" itself as the enemy. One of our editors recently gave birth to a child, and she simply cannot contemplate bringing that child up in a world without any economic growth.

Below we suggest ways in which Japan can contribute to resolving the crisis in global capitalism and to creating an ideal form of capitalism out of the currently existing many different forms.

For the 42 years since 1968, Japan was the world's second largest economic power after the United States until China overtook it this year [2010]. By 2020, India will probably also overtake Japan. Should Japan's citizens feel despondent about this?

No. The essential point is not quantity, but quality. We should be proud not of the scale of a country's GDP [gross domestic product], but rather of GDP per capita and the amount of happiness per individual.

The Japanese Virtues

In the first place, what position has Japan been given in world history? One important point is the historical meaning of Japan's being the first country to succeed in making a free capitalist economic society in the non-Western world. How was Japan able to do this?

Edward Morse, who came to Japan in 1877, was a professor at the University of Tokyo and is known as the discoverer of the Omori Shell Mounds. In his book *Japan Day by Day* on his impressions of Japan at that time, he wrote: "Japanese people are born with a politeness in behavior marked with virtue and character, and sensitivity towards others' feelings, the burden of moral training, dubbed 'humanity.'"

Morse stressed that "not only the well-off ranks but even the poorest people have these same traits." Many other Westerners who visited Japan around this time were also impressed by the "openness," "affinity" and "civility" of Japan.

Personal honor from an ethical viewpoint rather than based on material desires is the driving force behind Japan's development.

Open to and keenly interested in different kinds of civilization from their own, kind, and well-mannered—this is the vision of Japan that most contemporary foreigners had. Further, the view of many Westerners, as described by Isabella Bird, the Englishwoman who penned "Unbeaten Tracks in Japan," was: "As you can see from their attitude of being neither obsequious nor self-asserting, members of every class in Japan enjoy personal independence and freedom."

In his *Bushido: The Soul of Japan* written in English in the Meiji era, Inazo Nitobe proudly praised Japan's virtues to the world. The author saw the virtue and character possessed by the Japanese people as having their source in the Confucian teachings of the "Right Reason" as an absolute command, and "a sympathetic regard for the feelings of others" as an absolute virtue, while personal honor from an ethical viewpoint rather than based on material desires is the driving force behind Japan's development. He believed these values should be conserved as Japan's cultural heritage.

Representative Men of Japan, written in English by Kanzo Uchimura, mentions several enlightened Japanese leaders, including Uesugi Yozan, the strong leader of the Yonezawa clan who implemented fiscal reform in the late 18th century, and Ninomiya Sontoku, who conducted reform to improve production in Japan's poor agricultural villages.

An Ethical Economics

These figures, along with Adam Smith, share a high esteem for the power of morality and ethics in economic reform and for an independent spirit, as well as a disdain for financial support as a cause of idleness and avarice, and believe that a leader, in his or her parent-like position, should have high ideals; properly manage the people's independence, mutual assistance between neighbors, and national policies; and let the nation be one where diligence, love and independence rule. This ideal, especially in Uesugi's case, has something in common with former US President John Kennedy's famous words, "Ask not what your country can do for you . . . ask what you can do for your country."

These kinds of idealistic traditions were background factors in the economic development of Japan, the first non-Western modern country in the 20th century to be based on a free-market economy, in a similar way to how the origin of the philosophical foundation of Western capitalism can be seen as lying in Puritanism.

Nowadays, when a kind of capitalism different from Adam Smith's, one that can be called unethical and greedy, has broken down through the financial crisis and new forms of capitalism are being sought, showing the world Japan's original capitalism, based on its national identity, could make an important contribution.

The "openness," "affinity" and "civility" mentioned by Morse, and the "individual independence and freedom" found by Bird are surely Japan's model of democracy, built on the basis of the "Right Reason" and "a sympathetic regard for the feelings of others" that Nitobe boasted of and "stressing the power of morality and ethics as elements in economic reform" expressed by Uchimura; that is, a "capitalism with a caring spirit," so different from the dog-eats-dog type of capitalism, is Japan's true identity.

As "a state with a high degree of satisfaction based on people helping one another," shouldn't Japan also aim to be "a responsible country overflowing with civility and kindness?" With the government and the people both carrying out the responsibility to attain a high degree of happiness, built on the satisfaction of the people, Japan would then be a truly responsible, high-quality country that could help other countries.

This type of "Japan model" of capitalism is actually not so far from the thinking of traditional economics. We have stressed "independence and kindness" as characteristics of the Japan model, but traditional economic theory also has human beings with such features as its core assumption. The Japan model of capitalism can in fact be considered close to Adam Smith's capitalism.

The Welfare Economics

When discussing the desirable future form of capitalism, how the "roles of the market and the government" should be allotted is a core concern. The "welfare economics," a research field of traditional economics, holds the following view.

Originally, in the capitalist economy that assumes a market mechanism with individualism and personal responsibility, it was sufficient for the government only to streamline the economic environment such as law and order so the market could function fully while the government itself did not need to conduct economic activities. However, in the actual economy, the market mechanism also has demerits and, in response, welfare economics expects the government to fulfill the following four functions.

First, the government should provide "public goods" such as medical services which, if left entirely to the private sector, will not reach socially desirable levels due to insufficient profits.

Second, if things are left to the market, society is not necessarily able to realize an ideal allotment of income as a whole in the presence of differences in terms of asset ownership from the start. Therefore, the government should redistribute income through taxation.

Third, the government should play the role of stabilizing the business cycle through fiscal and monetary policies from a macroeconomic perspective.

What characterizes Japan's capitalism is for each member of society to have a "spirit of independence" so that individuals do not overly depend on the welfare policies.

Fourth, in the long term, the government should implement policies that consider benefits for future generations (for example, public infrastructure and the education system).

Clearly, the "Japan model" of capitalism is the most appropriate for the kind of society this type of welfare economics seeks. All four functions mentioned above are for the public benefit of society as a whole. "Civility and ethics," the foundation of "caring," can be seen as playing the greatest role in fostering this public spirit common to the four functions. Meanwhile, what characterizes Japan's capitalism is for each member of society to have a "spirit of independence" so that individuals do not overly depend on the welfare policies of a society based on the caring and public spirits.

A "welfare state" by itself often tends to result in moral hazard on the part of people, and may also bring about a lack of innovation, the driving force of the economy. Amid an in-

The Japanese Model of Capitalism

The idea of a middle way that can act as a model for other countries is seductive. "A lot of Asian countries are saying: 'We hope Japan will succeed, so we have a new model that combines capitalism with social values,'" says Hirotaka Takeuchi of Hitotsubashi University. Does that mean it is something like the European model? Yes, but not identical, because taxes are lower and the state is smaller in Japan— and unlike in France, Germany or Scandinavia, companies provide a lot of social support.

Economist,
"JapAnglo-Saxon Capitalism," vol. 385, no. 8557,
December 1, 2007.

creasingly aging society, the Japan model is intended to bring about a kind of welfare state that does not have these negative effects.

Advancing Social Welfare

The first policy issue is the realization of "advanced welfare," which relates mainly to the function of providing public goods. It has three aspects.

The first aspect is the tackling of aging, now a worldwide phenomenon, in a pioneering manner. Japan, which will experience an aged society first, should provide a world model of social welfare in measures to cope with aging as a nation able to fuse economic strength and ethical kindness.

In doing so, it should be emphasized that these measures are clearly meant to further individual independence. For example, there could be a system where "everyone is independent and can approach old age without worry." The minimum pension level could be raised to the world's highest level.

Meanwhile, for those with high income, benefits could be reduced in a gradated way. For people able to live alone, local municipalities would provide support for independence while care facilities would be provided for those unable to live alone, thus offering an environment where they could live without worry regardless of personal wealth. We must also further improve the quality of nursing-care insurance. Creating a non-discriminatory, gender-free, age-free society will increase employment opportunities for the elderly.

Second is a comprehensive response to the trend toward having fewer children. The future of Japan depends on the imagination and ability to act of today's children. We must expand the child-raising infrastructure (provide just the right number of child-care facilities), reduce child-raising costs (child benefits plus free education up until high school, but only for households with less than a certain income level), and improve the working environment for child-rearing people. . . .

For advanced welfare, a certain burden cannot be avoided, but this burden does not necessarily have to be large.

The third aspect is a broad-ranging response to unemployment, implementing a thorough unemployment safety net and occupational training for those unable to find work. For example, this could mean improving unemployment insurance linked to occupational training, including for temporary employees; strengthening national support for smooth labor transfer utilizing private-sector reemployment support companies; and especially strengthening the fostering of personnel in growth fields such as the environment, tourism, nursing/medical care, and high value-added agriculture.

Exploiting only one of these three factors is not enough. All must be fulfilled, using a balanced approach. For advanced welfare, a certain burden cannot be avoided, but this burden does not necessarily have to be large. While realizing high growth, a taxation system that enables advanced welfare with a medium-sized burden is essential.

Other Policies of Capitalism with Caring

In the following public policy issues, the coming generations should be duly considered.

The next policy issue after "advanced social welfare" is "maintaining advanced dynamic power." An aging society does not have to mean reduced dynamic power. Even as aging advances, we should aim to maintain strong industrial competitiveness, thus enabling advanced welfare with a medium-sized burden. . . .

The third public policy issue is to improve the quality of life. This requires us to establish a reputation among foreigners that Japan is a pleasant country to visit, invest in and live in. . . .

In order to realize the public policies mentioned above, it is essential to develop "capitalism with a caring spirit" which will spring from harmony between Japan-style ethical kindness and the market mechanism. And, for this Japan model of capitalism to contribute to the stability and prosperity of the global economy, . . . Japan's "high-level contributions" as a "state with responsibility" are important. These contributions entail turning around the traditional concept of "world peace and stability, and the economic prosperity that underpins them" to a Japanese style of "supporting economic prosperity and then establishing peace and stability on the basis of that precondition.". . .

During the last decade, there has been criticism of Japan as a "withdrawn" or an "introverted" country. In this time of crisis, it is important for Japan, the world's third largest economic power, to properly listen to such criticisms and, as a "state with responsibility," to offer this Japanese-style model of capitalism to the world.

In Canada, the Welfare System Has Masked the Problems with Capitalism

Ellen Russell, Wilfrid Laurier University

In the following viewpoint, Ellen Russell argues that nostalgia for the welfare state in Canada relies on a misplaced endorsement of the current capitalist market economy. Russell contends that the former Canadian welfare system relied on a redistributive system that has problems of divisiveness. Russell claims that instead of calling for a return to the welfare state, Canadians should be questioning the value of the market economy that produces vast inequalities. Russell is senior research economist at the Canadian Centre for Policy Alternatives.

As you read, consider the following questions:

1. The author refers to the good old days when Canadians used to hold what belief about government?

2. The author contends that the welfare state paradigm of a generation ago was predicated on what idea?

3. The author suggests that rather than relying on government to improve on the current economic system, it would be better to have what kind of system?

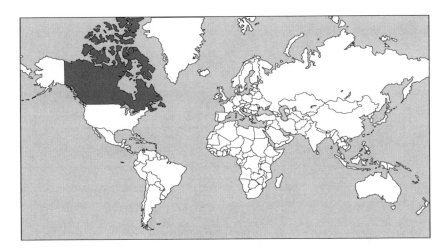

Remember the good old days when Canadians used to think the government was supposed to help everyone share in economic prosperity and prevent anyone from shouldering the brunt of economic adversity? We thought we'd learned the bitter lessons about the perils of the free market from the Great Depression. A welfare state was needed to moderate the harsh forces of the market, with government programs that entitle all citizens to certain social and economic rights.

Nostalgia for the Welfare State

Today, the welfare state programs of the 1960s and 1970s seem like a distant memory. Free marketeers have attacked everything from employment insurance to welfare to education funding.

One response of progressives to the shredding of the social safety net is the impulse to go back to where we were before the bad stuff happened. Remember the good old days, when most unemployed people could actually qualify for unemployment insurance? When the discussion was about how to fix or improve public services, not what price the government could get for auctioning them off? After losing so many fights over the decades to protect social programs, you can appreciate this nostalgia for the way things used to be. Wouldn't it be great to have adequate income support programs again instead of having to rely on the not-so-tender mercies of seedy payday loan joints?

But nostalgia for the past overstates the virtues of the welfare state. Carleton University sociologist Janet Siltanen's research shows that—even on its best days—the welfare state paradigm was far from paradise. Even in the "golden age" of the Canadian welfare state, politicians were long on rhetoric and short on substance. Income security programs were modest, and social programs were often not extended to everyone. Plus, a weak commitment to full employment meant that the Canadian government fell far short of placing the rights of citizens above market forces.

Nostalgia for the past overstates the virtues of the welfare state.

An Agenda of Redistribution

Some might argue that—despite its flaws—the Canadian welfare state of a generation ago is still preferable to today's neoliberal nightmare. But Siltanen argues that viewing the welfare state with rose-coloured glasses is not a great starting point for a new vision for Canada.

The welfare state paradigm was predicated on an agenda of redistribution: the idea that the government should take from the affluent to help out those who are struggling.

Under such a redistribution scheme, socially marginalized groups must fight over whose agendas will be supported from a limited pot of tax revenues. Groups that battle racism, sexism, homophobia or other forms of discrimination are badly disadvantaged when it comes to determining who are the deserving beneficiaries. For them, the welfare state is not a paradise lost.

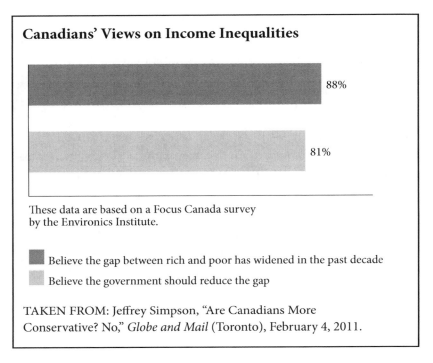

Canadians' Views on Income Inequalities

88%

81%

These data are based on a Focus Canada survey
by the Environics Institute.

■ Believe the gap between rich and poor has widened in the past decade

Believe the government should reduce the gap

TAKEN FROM: Jeffrey Simpson, "Are Canadians More
Conservative? No," *Globe and Mail* (Toronto), February 4, 2011.

Not that redistribution is a bad thing—far from it. And maybe we could sort out our oppressive prejudices enough to ensure that welfare state programs are not designed around the heterosexual-male-breadwinner household, and to ensure that many more groups (women and First Nations come to mind) receive the benefit of this redistributive vision.

> *If the economy weren't creating such gulfs between rich and poor, there would be less damage for the government to fix.*

Questioning the Economic System Itself

But there are other problems with welfare-state-style income redistribution as a political agenda. Taking from the haves and giving to the have-nots occludes a bigger question: Why is it that the economy *produces* haves and have-nots?

This is a question about more than just income redistribution. Rather than relying solely on government to try to improve on an economic system that reinforces inequality, wouldn't it be better if we had a more egalitarian economic system? If the economy weren't creating such gulfs between rich and poor, there would be less damage for the government to fix.

This line of reasoning leads in a number of interesting directions—directions we don't pursue if we are stuck in the past with the same redistribution mind-set we had a generation ago. Siltanen poses her own provocative question: Who said markets are sacred? The market economy, with all of its imperfections, is not some force of nature; it is socially created. So for Siltanen and others, we should not just set our sights on a return to some imaginary, glorious past, but on creating a future where the economic system itself is up for debate.

Iran Is Experiencing an Ongoing Struggle Between Welfare Spending and Privatization

Rostam Pourzal

In the following viewpoint, Rostam Pourzal claims that Iran has been engaged in a struggle between welfare spending and capitalist free market policies for decades. Pourzal explains how Iran's oil industry has been under government control through several political upheavals, including a revolution, with no sign of a change to privatization. Pourzal contends that opposition to government deregulation of the oil industry has come from different political camps over the years, but still shows no signs of immediate change. Pourzal is an independent researcher and organizer for human rights.

As you read, consider the following questions:

1. Pourzal claims that the campaign to downsize government in Iran centers on controversy about what?
2. According to the author, what event in 1980 increased the government's command of the economy?

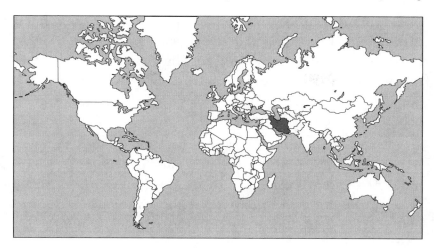

3. Pourzal contends that both public opinion and the bureaucracy in Iran are polarized about the relative merits of what two ways forward?

The last time skyrocketing oil prices tripled Iran's state budget, in the mid 1970s, a revolution followed that ended nearly a century of intrusion by foreign business giants. Under the banner of cultural authenticity and with overwhelming popular approval that united middle and working classes, the leadership of the new Islamic Republic massively enlarged the country's public sector and otherwise moved away from the Western business-friendly policies of the Shah. This policy shift has largely continued in the years since. The Heritage Foundation, a conservative think tank proudly devoted to the legacy of [former president] Ronald Reagan, yearly ranks Iran almost at the bottom among 157 nations in its "Index of Economic Freedom."

Iran's Oil Revenues

Now, a second oil windfall—expected to pump as much as $100 billion into the Iranian economy this year [2008]—is fueling a backlash. This time, though, it is the state's intrusion in the economy that is drawing ire among some Iranians and, unlike in 1979, polarizing public opinion along class lines. Massive social spending and state ownership of thousands of companies irritate the growing middle class, which feels that its interests have been subordinated to welfare and jobs programs long enough and now increasingly supports a range of neoliberal "free market" policies.

Campaigns to downsize government often target taxation, but in Iran the controversy centers on the country's vast oil industry, the fourth largest in the world. Oil exports currently provide roughly three-quarters of the national budget and make the state the largest player in the national economy. As a result, rapid hikes in oil revenue sow dissension in sectors of the public that do not see themselves enjoying a commensurate rise in living standards. (Of course, the tightening of U.S.-led international trade sanctions against Iran may be hobbling the government's attempts to use oil revenues to reduce poverty and meet social needs, but reliable data on the sanctions' effects are not available, and the government denies any impact.)

Massive social spending and state ownership of thousands of companies irritate the growing middle class.

Today, state coffers are overflowing, and extravagant consumption by political elites points to corruption in high places. In this context, some Iranians perceive the failure of President Mahmoud Ahmadinejad's administration to reduce the country's persistent double-digit unemployment rate as a glaring failure of "big government." This, and the frustration felt by Iranians whose gains from record oil revenue are offset by runaway inflation, are exploited by the "reformist" opposition, which blames social inequities on government mishandling of the economy and touts privatization and deregulation as solutions.

An Economic Policy Debate

Ahmadinejad is the object of middle-class ire because of fear that his populist programs have weakened the electoral chances of the neoliberal "reform" parties. Although he was a relative unknown beyond Tehran [Iran's capital city] before he ran for president in 2005, he easily beat his widely distrusted fiscal-conservative rival, former two-term president Hashemi Rafsanjani. Since taking office, Ahmadinejad has hiked subsidies on dozens of consumer necessities—from health care and books to food staples and electricity—to unprecedented levels. But his prospects for re-election next year [Ahmadinejad was re-elected president in 2009] are uncertain, as his parliamentary allies and even some cabinet-level officials are abandoning him for his refusal to shrink the government.

The push to shrink the public sector and cut social spending is ironic at a time when Iran's government has been taking in record oil revenues. If anything, the high unemployment and growing income inequality that the fiscal conservatives cite as proof of government incompetence will worsen with deregulation. The neoliberal push for privatization, however, may get a boost from the current decline in oil revenues, as world oil prices drop due to expectations of a global recession. A reduction in the resources available to the government to redistribute through its populist programs may weaken its support among the lower classes and strengthen the neoliberals. A bonanza would await private investors when oil prices rise again, as they almost certainly will in the medium to long run.

It may come as a surprise to consumers of the U.S. mainstream media that these economic policy debates are center stage in Iran's hotly contested presidential election next summer. Most U.S. media accounts characterize Iranian politics as a simple struggle between Ahmadinejad and his "extremist" camp, on the one hand, and "reformers" like Rafsanjani and Mohammad Khatami, on the other. As for the focus of the struggle, the media likewise point simplistically to either "tradition" versus "freedom" in the religious and cultural spheres, or to a "pro-U.S." versus "anti-U.S." stance in international relations. But Iran's politics reflect a complicated web of conflicting class interests that, in the years since the 1979 revolution, different leadership factions have at times both played to and genuinely addressed.

> *If anything, the high unemployment and growing income inequality that the fiscal conservatives cite as proof of government incompetence will worsen with deregulation.*

The Enlargement of Government Control

The economy that the Islamic Republic inherited in 1979 already had a sizable centralized public sector. Under the Pahlavi monarchy, publicly owned monopolies included the national airline, radio and television, railroads, port facilities, water and electric utilities, steel, tobacco, and telecommunications. Most important, Iran's oil was fully nationalized. In 1973, Shah Mohammad Reza Pahlavi had terminated the concessionary arrangement under which a consortium of U.S., British, Dutch, and French oil companies had run the Iranian oil industry since 1954—an arrangement the Shah himself had negotiated when he was reinstalled following the 1953 U.S.—and U.K. [United Kingdom]—instigated coup against nationalist prime minister Mohammad Mosaddegh. Moreover, privatization of the country's oil industry was nowhere on the political radar screen. When the quadrupling of oil prices in 1973–74 (the first "OPEC [Organization of the Petroleum Exporting Countries] oil shock") strengthened the Shah's rule, no element of the popular forces that chafed under his tyranny—not even the powerful merchant network that would finance the revolution—campaigned for privatization.

After the Shah fled, major assets that belonged to him and his allies or to his favored international investors were nationalized, along with all private banks. Vast religious endowments that he had not been able to take away from the clerical establishment also came under government control. These steps enlarged the public sector, as did massive social welfare and rural infrastructure programs that the new regime soon initiated. These programs represented a nod to the poor, who had been among the revolution's most active supporters. But the expropriations and growth in public spending found widespread support among all but a narrow slice of very affluent Iranians.

The U.S.-backed Iraqi invasion of Iran in 1980 and the eight-year war that ensued led to rationing and wartime reallocation of resources, which further increased the government's command of the economy. The war also set the stage for certain kinds of economic populism. For instance, during eight years of devastating conflict, standing up for private property rights while Iran's least prosperous families sacrificed sons and funds to defend the country would have seemed treasonous. So in thousands of cases, the government postponed evicting tenants and sharecroppers who stopped paying rent to their landlords following the revolution.

Opposition to the Revolutionary Regime

Populist economic policies, however, did not betoken government support for independent left political forces. By the time the war with Iraq ended in 1988, Iran had lost hundreds of thousands of its most productive citizens and had to provide for the disabled and displaced without international help. An unprecedented baby boom and over a million refugees from war-torn Afghanistan also strained the government's resources. Moving to consolidate its power and stem any instability, that year the government executed hundreds—by some accounts thousands—of suspected Communist opposition members who had languished in prison since roundups earlier in the decade. They, along with thousands of other progressives who fled abroad during the Iraq war, had been vocal opponents of the Shah, but had increasingly come to oppose the revolutionary regime as it became more uniformly Islamist and theocratic.

Upper-income Iranians' support for the regime waned as well, albeit for very different reasons. Their doubts flowed in part from discriminatory policies favoring government loyalists, some of whom helped crack down on civil liberties. Preferential treatment included set-aside quotas in college admissions and employment for disadvantaged war veterans and their families.

Rafsanjani's economic agenda was widely resisted and ultimately unsuccessful.

In the aftermath of the Iraq war, populist economic policies were newly vulnerable. During the 1990s, President Rafsanjani pushed for changes to labor, banking, and property laws designed to attract foreign investment for reconstruction. With his encouragement, Iran's managerial class and business leaders and their academic allies argued that deregulation, privatization, and cuts in subsidies and public services were necessary to achieve the rapid economic growth that would best serve the masses.

However, Rafsanjani's economic agenda was widely resisted and ultimately unsuccessful. His harshest critics called it a counterrevolution, hinting that they suspected the neoliberal camp of loyalty to the Western "enemy," an accusation that has long resonated, especially with Iranians of modest means. Two key episodes in Iran's history have reinforced a link in Iranian public opinion between national sovereignty and the government's ability to regulate the market. In 1891, the Tobacco Revolt forced the cancellation of monopoly rights granted to a British entrepreneur. The 1953 overthrow of Mosaddegh, ousted because of his plan to nationalize Iran's oil, opened the country to a flood of foreign business ventures. Many Iranians, as a result, view concessions to corporate interests as inherently suspect, and policies creating an "open" business climate as a Trojan horse for disruptive globalization.

Polarization over Privatization

Today, both public opinion and the bureaucracy in Iran are polarized about the relative merits of an expanded state sector, with its focus on rewarding political loyalty and undertaking socioeconomic redistribution, versus "performance," "transparency," and "meritocracy," the buzzwords for privatization and deregulation. Thousands of official monuments, murals, and street names glorify the revolution's "martyrs"— implicitly calling on Iranians to put public interest above private gain. At the same time, political "moderates" dismiss appeals for economic fairness as outdated "ideology."

After simmering for years, the partisan disagreement is boiling over and splitting the electorate along class lines, as both sides mobilize for next summer's presidential election.

One flashpoint has been whether to remove the oil industry, and particularly oil revenues, from government control. Government opponents in sizeable numbers are demanding that the oil industry be privatized or else that oil revenue be channeled directly to "the people" without state mediation. According to them, the ruling social conservatives, who have vastly expanded Iran's social safety net and instituted affirmative action programs, are keeping the country backward with their anti–free market dogma. This camp points out that Iranian investors have flocked with billions of dollars to the booming free-trade haven of Dubai [in the United Arab Emirates] across the Persian Gulf and that the brain drain that has afflicted Iran for years shows no signs of slowing. On the other side are the mainly low- and moderate-income beneficiaries of the safety-net and affirmative-action programs— those for whom Ahmadinejad, the hands-on populist, symbolizes resistance to trickle-down economics and global free trade. They widely oppose oil industry privatization.

The contrast is evident at the leadership level. On the one hand, Ahmadinejad holds walk-in citizen request hours in the capital and well-attended rallies in the provinces where he routinely orders fast-track funding for grassroots initiatives. His closest international ally is Venezuelan President Hugo Chávez, perhaps the most prominent head of state identified with the World Social Forum movement. Ahmadinejad's immediate predecessor, reformist icon Mohammad Khatami, on the other hand, promotes his Dialog of Civilizations at the World Economic Forum in Davos, Switzerland, the glitzy annual gathering where business and political elites discuss strategies for further corporate globalization. And Hashemi Rafsanjani aggressively promotes the "invisible hand" of the market as head of the Expediency [Discernment] Council, the influential government body created in 1988 to resolve differences between the parliament and the senior clerics. Rafsanjani, too, takes well-publicized trips across the country a few times every year. But his purpose is usually to showcase a new campus of the pioneering Islamic Free University, a large chain of private colleges that he cofounded in the mid-1980s with state subsidies and that now enrolls well over a half million students nationwide.

The privatization plan leaves the fate of welfare spending, along with broader questions about the extent of state versus private power in the economy, to be settled through factional battles.

The Continuing Struggle

The Supreme Leader, Ayatollah Ali Khamenei, who has ultimate authority in Iran, walks a fine line and plays peacekeeper between the two factions in this as well as other contentious issues. Whereas Ahmadinejad has on at least one occasion used the word "socialism" to describe his economic agenda, Khamenei is on record calling for a "middle line between capitalism and socialism." (Ajmadinejad's "socialism," it must be noted, offers no more space for independent labor unions than does his critics' neoliberalism.)

The most likely outcome of the power struggle over the next decade and beyond is that each side will win a part of what it wants. The fiscal conservatives have needed someone with a cleaner reputation than Rafsanjani as the public face of privatization, and Khamenei is stepping in to fill that void. He may be making a virtue of necessity, though, because Iran's demographic winds are blowing in the direction of privatization. The country's middle class has expanded substantially since the 1970s and will grow even faster if the oil windfall continues. As it does, it will demand a greater share of the country's resources relative to the low-income beneficiaries of current government spending, a share that it cannot get unless power shifts from elected bodies to the less answerable corporate sector. In fact, considering how Khamanei spent seven years ordering the Expediency [Discernment] Council to prepare studies, revisions, and clarifications before he signed off on a privatization plan, it appears that his real intention may be to slow the privatization drive or limit its scope.

In interviews, Khamanei has called for privatization on the grounds that it would strengthen the nation, reduce poverty, and lessen corruption. But he does not necessarily use the term in the same way as the neoliberals do. For instance, he has labeled as "privatization" an Ahmadinejad initiative that has sold shares in industrial enterprises to millions of low-income families at a discount—a program dismissed as a populist gimmick by the president's neoliberal critics. At least for now, the privatization plan leaves the fate of welfare spending, along with broader questions about the extent of state versus private power in the economy, to be settled through factional battles.

Portugal's Welfare State Is Keeping It from Succeeding Economically

George Bragues

In the following viewpoint, George Bragues argues that Portugal's financial problems are not simply a problem of currency but are brought about by its attempt to create a welfare state. Bragues claims that the antiauthoritarian revolution over three decades ago created a social democracy with very large government expenditures that were never fully financed in any year, due to political unpopularity. He concludes that without adopting market reforms that move away from welfare, the country will not succeed. Bragues is the head of the business program at the University of Guelph-Humber in Toronto, Canada.

As you read, consider the following questions:

1. Bragues claims that Portugal's economy is in bad shape, but not as bad as what two other European Union countries?

2. How much did government spending, as a percentage of gross domestic product (GDP), increase after the 1974 revolution, according to the author?

3. According to Bragues, what has been an annual feature of government spending in Portugal every year since the revolution?

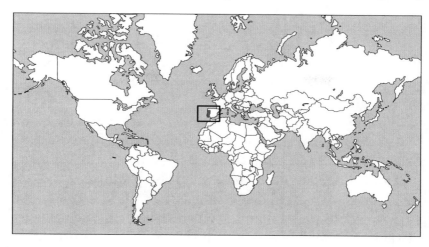

Portugal has suddenly become something of a player on the world stage, if for all the wrong reasons. With Ireland having gone the way of Greece in needing an IMF-EU [International Monetary Fund–European Union] bailout, the financial markets are betting that Portugal will be next. Though its banks are no way near in as bad shape as those in Ireland, and though its public debt/GDP [gross domestic product] ratio is well below that of Greece, bond traders have taken to record levels the yield spread on 10-year Portuguese government bonds versus the benchmark German bonds.

This cannot be explained away as an irrational contagion process abetted by so-called bond vigilantes. Portugal shows little sign of being able to generate the wealth necessary to manage its debt. It has suffered its own "lost decade" of anemic growth, while the competitiveness of its export sector has fallen. Noting that this has taken place over the same period that the country has been using the euro, many of those trying to make sense of the market's movements argue that investors have simply figured out that the European currency union puts countries like Portugal in a bind from which it cannot export its way out via an exchange-rate depreciation.

Portugal's Welfare State

Portugal's difficulties, though, run much deeper than the existing currency framework. Its problems are the culmination of a three-and-a-half decade project to erect a social-democratic welfare state.

That project evolved out of the 1974 Carnation Revolution that overthrew an authoritarian regime known as the New State ("Estado Novo" in Portuguese). Dominated by the figure of António de Oliveira Salazar, who ruled Portugal as a dictator from 1932 to 1968, the New State was officially committed to a corporativist economic system that envisioned the replacement of individualistic competition by the collaboration of vital social groups in production decisions.

Portugal's difficulties ... are the culmination of a three-and-a-half decade project to erect a social-democratic welfare state.

In practice, the Portuguese economy fell short of this ideal and so the revolutionaries of 1974 ended up confronting a state-directed capitalism privileging a narrow business elite loyal to the dictatorship. Numerous industries owned by this elite, starting with insurance and banking, were nationalized in the immediate aftermath of the uprising in what would become the first of a series of political acts to define the post-1974 economic structure.

Most critical among these acts was the 1976 constitution that established Portugal as a modern democracy. Its preamble affirmed the necessity of "opening a path to a socialist society," while entrenching the nationalizations undertaken after the revolution. Labour was constitutionally empowered, buttressing existing laws that make it extremely onerous to dismiss full-time workers.

Citizens were additionally granted a multitude of social and economic rights, including the right to work, housing, education, culture, health, and social security. These provisions were heeded by Portugal's political classes, as the state apparatus progressively grew to fulfill the newly assumed constitutional obligations. Prior to the 1974 revolution, the government spent about 20% of GDP [gross domestic product], mostly on the traditional functions of military defence, domestic administration, and infrastructure. Since then, driven by social expenditures, the weight of government has risen to 46% of GDP, higher than the European average. Over the same period, the number of public-sector workers quadrupled.

Unlike other developed nations, Portugal built its welfare state on a relatively weak economic foundation.

A Country of Debt

To anyone who remembers what Portugal was like in the 1970s and visits the country now, the economic progress that has been made is patently obvious. But its social-democratic experiment has delivered far less than meets the eye. It has never matched the growth rates witnessed from 1945–74, the best in Portugal's modern history, when the New State opened the country to foreign investment and trade. GDP per capita rose from 30% of the European average to 50%. After 1974, this figure reached 66% in 2000, but has since fallen back to 60%.

Not only has the convergence been smaller in the post-revolutionary period, it has been significantly purchased with the assumption of debt. Right from the start, both in 1978 and 1983, the IMF was brought in to deal with external imbalances. Since the 1990s, Portugal's current-account deficits have once again dangerously accumulated, thanks to high corporate and household borrowing.

By contrast, balance of payments troubles never arose during the New State while Salazar, formerly an economics professor of the pre-Keynesian [named after British economist

John Maynard Keynes] school, was consistently balancing the budget. But under the sway of Keynesian thinking, and with its politicians not daring to upset voters by imposing the taxes necessary to pay for the country's growing welfare state, Portugal has astonishingly never once managed to avoid a fiscal deficit in the 36 years since the revolution.

A Lack of Economic Freedom

With any debt-fuelled activity, the day of reckoning can take a while to arrive. In Portugal's case, it was delayed by the provision of limited-term work contracts, which attenuated the impact of its labour laws. Even so, the rigidity of these is still very great by world standards, deterring the capital investment needed to raise productivity. During the 1980s, too, the constitution was amended to allow the privatization of previously nationalized firms. Combined with Portugal's entry into the EU in 1986, this reflected a shift toward free markets that, up until the early 1990s, led the country to its best economic performance of the post-revolutionary era.

Alas, this turn proved ephemeral, as Portugal's ranking in the Heritage Foundation economic freedom index fell from 38th place in 1995 to its current standing at 62nd. The country's adoption of the euro also bought some time by reducing debt-servicing costs. Figuring that giving up its own currency would force the government to implement market reforms, instead of resorting to the previous ways of depreciation, the bond market lowered the risk premium charged on Portuguese debt. But few reforms were made.

Unlike other developed nations, Portugal built its welfare state on a relatively weak economic foundation. Hence, it is among the first to have run into difficulties, making it a harbinger of the coming crack-up in social democracy. What Portugal can, and must, do is show the way out of this morass by truly completing its revolution and extending the freedom that its people won in the political sphere to their economic lives as well.

Periodical and Internet Sources Bibliography

The following articles have been selected to supplement the diverse views presented in this chapter.

Josep María Antentas and Esther Vivas	"The New Chinese Capitalism," *IV Online*, September 2008. www.internationalviewpoint.org.
Mona Charen	"Stand Up for Capitalism!," *National Review Online*, March 6, 2009. www.nationalreview.com.
Economist	"Europe and America: Lessons from a Crisis," October 2, 2008.
Economist	"JapAnglo-Saxon Capitalism," November 29, 2007.
Richard W. Fulmer	"The Paradox of the Welfare State," *Freeman*, October 2010.
Ilan Greenberg	"Children of the Revolution: Why Does Greece Still Have Left-Wing Terrorists?," *Foreign Policy*, November 12, 2010. www.foreignpolicy.com.
George Hara	"Enriching Lives of People in Developing Countries Through Public Interest Capitalism," *Japan Spotlight: Economy, Culture, and History*, November/December 2009.
Steven Hill	"The Trans-Atlantic Clash over Political Economy and Fulcrum Institutions," *Social Europe Journal*, Winter 2008.
Michael Rustin	"Contradictions in the Contemporary Welfare State," *Soundings*, Spring 2008.
Peter Smith	"The Economics of Hope and Despair," *Quadrant*, January/February 2011.

For Further Discussion

Chapter 1

1. In this chapter's viewpoints, what countries are identified as having popular opinion in favor of capitalism? What countries are identified as having popular opinion against capitalism? Use specific text to back up your answers.

Chapter 2

1. Among the authors of the viewpoints in this chapter, what is the main point of disagreement about the relationship between capitalism and the global financial crisis? Give an example of two opposing viewpoints between two authors.

2. Kevin Rudd speaks of the "middle way" between state socialism and free market fundamentalism. What other author(s) endorse this kind of blend of capitalism and state regulation?

Chapter 3

1. In this chapter, authors of the viewpoints take different stances on the relationship between capitalism and democracy. Which author(s) believes capitalism and democracy are compatible? Which author(s) believes capitalism and democracy are incompatible? Which author(s) believes capitalism and democracy do not need the other to exist? Use specific quotations of each author to back up your answer.

Chapter 4

1. According to the authors of the viewpoints in this chapter, what countries currently combine capitalism with generous welfare spending?

2. Name at least one argument from one of the viewpoints in this chapter against coupling capitalism with welfare spending. Name at least one argument from one of the viewpoints in this chapter in favor of coupling capitalism with welfare spending. Which is the stronger argument in your opinion?

Organizations to Contact

The editors have compiled the following list of organizations concerned with the issues debated in this book. The descriptions are derived from materials provided by the organizations. All have publications or information available for interested readers. The list was compiled on the date of publication of the present volume; the information provided here may change. Be aware that many organizations take several weeks or longer to respond to inquiries, so allow as much time as possible.

Adam Smith Institute
23 Great Smith Street, London   SW1P 3BL
  United Kingdom
(44) 20 7222 4995
e-mail: info@adamsmith.org
website: www.adamsmith.org

The Adam Smith Institute is a libertarian think tank in the United Kingdom. Through its research, education programs, and media appearances, it promotes free markets, limited government, and an open society. The Adam Smith Institute publishes articles and reports, such as "Reflections on Regulation: Experience and the Future."

American Enterprise Institute for Public
Policy Research (AEI)
1150 Seventeenth Street NW, Washington, DC   20036
(202) 862-5800 • fax: (202) 862-7177
e-mail: info@aei.org
website: www.aei.org

The American Enterprise Institute for Public Policy Research (AEI) is a private, nonpartisan, nonprofit institution dedicated to research and education on issues of government, politics, economics, and social welfare. AEI sponsors research and publishes materials toward the end of defending the principles and improving the institutions of American freedom and democratic capitalism. AEI publishes the *American*, a bimonthly magazine.

Ayn Rand Institute (ARI)

2121 Alton Parkway, Suite 250, Irvine, CA 92606-4926
(949) 222-6550 • fax: (949) 222-6558
website: www.aynrand.org

The Ayn Rand Institute (ARI) seeks to spearhead a cultural renaissance in an attempt to reverse the anti-reason, anti-individualism, anti-freedom, anti-capitalist trends it perceives in today's culture. ARI works to introduce young people to Ayn Rand's novels; to support scholarship and research based on her ideas; and to promote the principles of reason, rational self-interest, individual rights, and laissez-faire capitalism to the widest possible audience. The institute publishes information on objectivism, including "Capitalism: The Unknown Ideal."

Cato Institute

1000 Massachusetts Avenue NW
Washington, DC 20001-5403
(202) 842-0200 • fax: (202) 842-3490
website: www.cato.org

The Cato Institute is a public policy research foundation dedicated to limiting the role of government, protecting individual liberties, and promoting free markets. The Cato Institute works to originate, advocate, promote, and disseminate applicable policy proposals that create free, open, and civil societies in the United States and throughout the world. Among the Cato Institute's publications is the *Cato Policy Report*, which includes articles such as "Capitalism and Human Nature."

Center for the Advancement of Capitalism

PO Box 221462, Chantilly, VA 20153-1462

e-mail: info@capitalismcenter.org
website: www.capitalismcenter.org

The Center for the Advancement of Capitalism is dedicated to advancing individual rights and economic freedom. The center engages in legal advocacy and business advocacy in support of capitalistic principles. Numerous essays are available at the center's website, including "The Moral Basis of Capitalism."

Centre for Economic Policy Research (CEPR)

77 Bastwick Street, 3rd floor, London   ECIV 3PZ
United Kingdom
(44) 20 7183 8801 • fax: (44) 20 7183 8820
e-mail: cepr@cepr.org
website: www.cepr.org

The Centre for Economic Policy Research (CEPR) is the leading European research network in economics. CEPR conducts research through a network of academic researchers and disseminates the results to the private sector and policy community. CEPR produces a wide range of reports, books, and conference volumes each year, including "The First Global Financial Crisis of the 21st Century."

Economic Policy Institute (EPI)

1333 H Street NW, Suite 300, East Tower
Washington, DC   20005-4707
(202) 775-8810 • fax: (202) 775-0819
e-mail: epi@epi.org
website: www.epi.org

The Economic Policy Institute (EPI) is a nonprofit Washington, DC, think tank that seeks to broaden the discussion about economic policy to include the interests of low- and middle-income workers. EPI briefs policy makers at all levels of government; provides technical support to national, state, and local activists and community organizations; testifies before national, state, and local legislatures; and provides information and background to the print and electronic media. EPI publishes books, studies, issue briefs, popular education materials, and other publications, among which is the biennially published *State of Working America.*

Global Policy Forum (GPF)

777 UN Plaza, Suite 3D, New York, NY 10017
(212) 557-3161 • fax: (212) 557-3165
e-mail: gpf@globalpolicy.org
website: www.globalpolicy.org

Global Policy Forum (GPF) is a nonprofit organization with consultative status at the United Nations (UN). The mission of GPF is to monitor policy making at the UN, promote accountability of global decisions, educate and mobilize for global citizen participation, and advocate on vital issues of international peace and justice. GPF publishes policy papers, articles, and statements, including the briefing paper "Some Reflections on the Current Global Crisis from a Developing Countries Perspective."

Institute for America's Future (IAF)

1825 K Street NW, Suite 400, Washington, DC 20006
(202) 955-5665 • fax: (202) 955-5606
website: http://institute.ourfuture.org

The Institute for America's Future (IAF) works to equip Americans with the tools and information needed to drive issues into the national debate, challenge failed conservative policies, and build support for the progressive vision of a government that is on the side of working people. Drawing on a network of scholars, activists, and leaders across the country, IAF develops policy ideas, educational materials, and outreach programs. Publications of IAF include "The Financial Crisis and Crony Capitalism."

International Monetary Fund (IMF)

700 Nineteenth Street NW, Washington, DC 20431
(202) 623-7000 • fax: (202) 623-4661

e-mail: publicaffairs@imf.org
website: www.imf.org

The International Monetary Fund (IMF) is an organization of 186 countries working to foster global monetary cooperation, secure financial stability, facilitate international trade, promote high employment and sustainable economic growth, and reduce poverty around the world. The IMF monitors the world's economies, lends to members in economic difficulty, and provides technical assistance. The IMF publishes fact sheets, reports on key issues, and the *IMF Annual Report.*

International Trade Union Confederation (ITUC)

5 Boulevard du Roi Albert II, Bte 1, Brussels   1210
   Belgium
(32) 2 224 0211 • fax: (32) 2 201 5815
e-mail: info@ituc-csi.org
website: www.ituc-csi.org

The International Trade Union Confederation (ITUC) is an international advocacy group for trade unions, supporting their mission to improve working conditions. The ITUC promotes and defends workers' rights and interests through international cooperation between trade unions, global campaigning, and advocacy within the major global institutions. Available at the ITUC's website are various publications and reports, including "Where the House Always Wins—Private Equity, Hedge Funds, and the New Casino Capitalism."

Peter G. Peterson Institute for International Economics

1750 Massachusetts Avenue NW
Washington, DC   20036-1903
(202) 328-9000 • fax: (202) 659-3225
e-mail: comments@petersoninstitute.org
website: www.iie.com

The Peter G. Peterson Institute for International Economics is a private, nonprofit, nonpartisan research institution devoted to the study of international economic policy. The institute seeks to provide timely and objective analysis of and concrete solutions to a wide range of international economic problems. The institute publishes numerous policy briefs available at its website, including "How Europe Can Muddle Through Its Crisis."

Socialist Alternative

PO Box 150457, Brooklyn, NY   11215
(718) 207-4037
e-mail: info@socialistalternative.org
website: www.socialistalternative.org

Socialist Alternative is a national organization fighting against the global capitalist system. Socialist Alternative campaigns for the building of a workers' party to represent the interests of workers, youth, and the environment against what it sees as the two parties of big business. Among the publications available at its website is the paper "Why You Should Be a Socialist."

Bibliography of Books

Brian C. Anderson
Democratic Capitalism and Its Discontents. Wilmington, DE: ISI Books, 2007.

Joyce Appleby
The Relentless Revolution: A History of Capitalism. New York: W.W. Norton, 2010.

Dean Baker
The Conservative Nanny State: How the Wealthy Use the Government to Stay Rich and Get Richer. Washington, DC: Center for Economic and Policy Research, 2006.

Benjamin R. Barber
Con$umed: How Markets Corrupt Children, Infantilize Adults, and Swallow Citizens Whole. New York: W.W. Norton, 2007.

John C. Bogle
The Battle for the Soul of Capitalism. New Haven, CT: Yale University Press, 2005.

Ian Bremmer
The End of the Free Market: Who Wins the War Between States and Corporations? New York: Portfolio, 2010.

Ha-Joon Chang
23 Things They Don't Tell You About Capitalism. New York: Allen Lane, 2010.

Thomas G. Donlan
A World of Wealth: How Capitalism Turns Profits into Progress. Upper Saddle River, NJ: FT Press, 2008.

232

Margarita
Estévez-Abe

Welfare and Capitalism in Postwar Japan. New York: Cambridge University Press, 2008.

Jeffry A. Frieden

Global Capitalism: Its Fall and Rise in the Twentieth Century. New York: W.W. Norton, 2007.

David Gratzer

The Cure: How Capitalism Can Save American Health Care. New York: Encounter Books, 2006.

Steven Hill

Europe's Promise: Why the European Way Is the Best Hope in an Insecure Age. Berkeley: University of California Press, 2010.

Naomi Klein

The Shock Doctrine: The Rise of Disaster Capitalism. New York: Metropolitan Books/Henry Holt, 2007.

John R. Lott Jr.

Freedomnomics: Why the Free Market Works and Other Half-Baked Theories Don't. Washington, DC: Regnery Publishing, 2007.

Robert P. Murphy

The Politically Incorrect Guide to Capitalism. Washington, DC: Regnery Publishing, 2007.

Vali Nasr

The Rise of Islamic Capitalism: Why the New Muslim Middle Class Is the Key to Defeating Extremism. New York: Free Press, 2010.

Richard A. Posner

A Failure of Capitalism: The Crisis of '08 and the Descent into Depression. Cambridge, MA: Harvard University Press, 2009.

Robert B. Reich	*Supercapitalism: The Transformation of Business, Democracy, and Everyday Life*. New York: Alfred A. Knopf, 2008.
Jay W. Richards	*Money, Greed, and God: Why Capitalism Is the Solution and Not the Problem*. New York: HarperOne, 2009.
William I. Robinson	*Latin America and Global Capitalism: A Critical Globalization Perspective*. Baltimore, MD: Johns Hopkins University Press, 2008.
Michael Shermer	*The Mind of the Market: Compassionate Apes, Competitive Humans, and Other Tales from Evolutionary Economics*. New York: Times Books, 2008.
Thomas Sowell	*Applied Economics: Thinking Beyond Stage One*. New York: Basic Books, 2009.
Kellee S. Tsai	*Capitalism Without Democracy: The Private Sector in Contemporary China*. Ithaca, NY: Cornell University Press, 2007.
Thomas E. Woods Jr.	*Meltdown: A Free-Market Look at Why the Stock Market Collapsed, the Economy Tanked, and Government Bailouts Will Make Things Worse*. Washington, DC: Regnery Publishing, 2009.

Index

Geographic headings and page numbers in **boldface** refer to viewpoints about that country or region.

S